CONTENTS

GILDA JOYCE
The Bones of the Holy

PROLOGUE

THE DREAM

Gilda walked through a jungle where animal
bones grew from the ground like trees. She
was on a quest to find someone, but she had
no path to follow--no map or clues.

She entered a clearing and found a moonlit
cemetery where a woman in white twirled and
danced beneath the moon. Gilda knew this
woman was not quite human. Her dark hair was
a shadow, her dress a ghostly whorl of smoke.

Amidst the tombstones, Gilda sensed
turbulence--the whispered arguments of trapped
spirits. Intermingling voices spoke in
different languages and old dialects--laughing,
crying, and arguing with one another.

"I'm looking for someone who's still
alive," Gilda said.

"In this place, the dead walk among the
living," said the phantom-woman.

A little bell rang, drawing Gilda's
attention to a wooden coffin that lay on the
ground. A knocking sound came from inside.
Struggling, Gilda managed to pry open the
coffin lid.

Her heart sank when she recognized her
mother's chalk-white face inside.

1

Spy Report

TO: GILDA JOYCE
FROM: GILDA JOYCE
RE: SPY REPORT

Okay--I know snooping in someone's
suitcase is wrong, but sometimes it's
also necessary. My reason for spying: Mom
suddenly announced that she's going on
something she called a "Mom's Getaway" trip
to Florida. That's right; she's heading for
the beach and leaving me and Stephen behind
in Michigan. I mean, I can understand
leaving my older brother behind. But me?!

"You mean to tell me, you're abandoning
us and heading for the Sunshine State?!" I
protested. "You're leaving two defenseless
teenagers to scrounge for scraps of lunch
meat in the city Dumpsters, while you burn
your freckles on some nude beach?"

"Very funny, Gilda," said Mom. (I admit
it: Mom is fun to tease because she never
has a good comeback.) "Anyway, it's just for
a short weekend," she explained. "You'll
survive without me for two days."

Mom had a point: I've been telling her
for years that I'm old enough to stay home
by myself. I also knew that it wasn't
really Mom's fault that I wasn't invited.
Her friend Lucy had won two flights to
Florida in a fund-raising raffle. Even so,
I was jealous, and I wasn't about to make
it easy for Mom to leave without me. "Some
parents might worry about leaving two
teenagers home alone," I said.

"I'll ask Grandma Joyce to come over and
check on you," Mom replied.

I wasn't too pleased about this since
Grandma Joyce has a way of turning a
perfectly fun pizza-and-a-movie night into
a tedious clean-up-the-whole-house night.
"That's okay," I sighed. "Grandma Joyce
doesn't need to come over. We'll be fine."

I suppose it's a little ironic that I'm
jealous of Mom's trip. I guess I always
assumed that if Mom ever went anywhere,
it would be to somewhere boring--perhaps
a bedpan-cleaning convention in Ohio or
a nineteenth-century slipper museum in

downtown Detroit. I never expected Mom
to announce a trip down to sunny Florida
without me!

Just then, the phone rang, and Mom
jumped up like a jackrabbit to answer it.
I noticed that she disappeared into the
hallway to take the call, which seemed a
little suspicious. While she was talking, I
took the opportunity to peek at some of the
clothes she had hidden at the bottom of her
suitcase. What I saw hidden under her beach
towel made me even more suspicious. NEW
things. A new black bathing suit instead
of her usual mom-style floral tankini-
with-attached-skirt. A new sundress with
matching sandals. Earrings and a necklace.
A toothbrush. DENTAL FLOSS. (Okay. I guess
those last items were normal enough for
Mom.) Still. Mom doesn't buy new things
very often since she's been saving money
to help pay for Stephen's room and board
at college next year. And she definitely
doesn't dress up just to see her friend
Lucy, whom she sees dressed in hospital
scrubs practically every day of the week.

I pressed my ear against the wall,
trying to hear what Mom was saying on the
phone. I couldn't make out any words, but
I heard the familiar nervous giggling that

usually signaled a first date. I've been
hearing it every few weeks, ever since Mom
joined that online dating service over the
summer, so I had a gut feeling Mom was
talking to a man--and not just a friend
either.

What is Mom up to? I wondered. What is
she hiding?

"Who was that?" I asked, trying to sound
nonchalant when Mom returned to finish
packing.

"Oh, just Lucy, reminding me to pack
some sunscreen."

"Are you SURE it was Lucy?"

"Why wouldn't it be Lucy?"

One thing I've learned in my career
as a spy and sleuth: When you confront a
person with something ("Did you steal my
sandwich?") and they answer your question
with another question (as in, "Why would I
want to steal your sandwich?"), the chances
are good that they actually DID the very
thing they're denying. Especially when
you're dealing with an inexperienced liar
like Mom.

As I stared at Mom's open suitcase,
watching her nervously fold and refold
clothes with her freshly manicured hands,

I distinctly felt a psychic signal--that
little tickle in my left ear I sometimes
get when something unusual is about to
happen. Sometimes it means there's spirit
activity in the area. Other times, it's a
premonition of danger.

I realize I have no proof, but I'm
almost certain that Mom is hiding something
about this trip to Florida. I just need to
figure out what and why.

2

The Sleepover

I dunno," said Wendy. "It looks kind of clownish."

Gilda and Wendy stared at Gilda's hair in the bathroom mirror. Wendy had been Gilda's best friend for years, and most often, Gilda appreciated Wendy's honesty. Other times, like now, it annoyed her.

The experiment with red hair dye hadn't turned out the way Gilda had hoped. She had imagined returning to school on Monday as a more interesting version of herself—a sultry, sophisticated, and intriguing redhead—and she figured her mother's absence for the weekend provided the perfect opportunity to attempt the experiment.

But this red looked far too bright, even for Gilda's adventurous taste. It looked as if she had dipped her hair into a pot of orange acrylic paint.

Wendy had bravely (and somewhat uncharacteristically) joined Gilda in the hair-dying experiment, but as it turned out, the red hair dye scarcely showed on her darker hair.

Gilda eyed Wendy's faintly auburn black hair with resentment. "Why isn't your hair red, too?" she demanded. "You must have cheated."

"Cheated how?"

"I don't know. You didn't put enough hair dye on there or something."

"I didn't realize we were having a contest to see who can look most like a Raggedy Ann doll," Wendy retorted.

"Well, we *were*. So there." Gilda considered her options: She could go back to the drugstore and buy a darker shade to cover the bright red. The problem was that she might not have enough money left in her purse to buy more hair dye after a weekend of movie theater and shopping mall excursions with Wendy.

"Hey," said Wendy as she clicked through some Internet links on her cell phone. "It says here on this Dye Your Own Hair website that grape Kool-Aid is supposed to tone down red hair color. It also says that if it's temporary hair color, it won't lighten dark hair like mine."

"Oh." Gilda squinted at the empty package of hair color. "I guess it would have been a good idea to read the directions first."

"You said you read them!"

"Well, I didn't read all the fine print. I read the quick 'n' easy steps."

"It's a good thing you aren't planning to be a surgeon or something."

"I doubt surgeons are sitting there reading the directions as they cut into people."

"You know what I mean." Wendy took the hair-color box out of Gilda's hand. "We're lucky this is temporary color."

"See? I knew what I was doing."

"It will wash out in about thirty shampoos."

"Thirty?! I don't have that kind of time. We'll have to try the Kool-Aid."

"So go down to the kitchen and get the Kool-Aid. Let's try it."

"We don't have any toddlers around here, Wendy. Now I have to ask Stephen to drive me to the store. Which means I'll never hear an end to the jokes about this."

"I could go with him," Wendy quickly offered.

A bit too quickly, Gilda thought, annoyed that Wendy still had a crush on her older brother. *Why does she even like him?* Gilda wondered. *Sure, he's tall and his skin has cleared up a lot lately. And I guess he acts more confident now that he's been accepted into college. Still, Wendy has no idea just how self-centered Stephen can be.*

Stephen and Wendy had gotten to know each other better at a math camp over the summer. While Stephen had felt a very secret spark of attraction to Wendy during their conversations about quantum mechanics, he maintained that she was "too young" for him, since he was a senior and she was only a sophomore. Besides, Wendy was his little sister's best friend. Nevertheless, Wendy harbored hope that Stephen would change his mind and see her as a potential girlfriend.

"I mean," Wendy added, "you could stay here so Stephen won't see your hair. I'll go with him and I can run into the store and pick up the Kool-Aid."

"I should have known this whole sleepover was just a ruse to see my geeky brother," Gilda complained.

"It's *not.* I'm just trying to help you solve this hair problem."

Wendy tapped on her cell phone again. "Stephen's at work now, right?"

"Probably just finishing."

"So I'll just call him and see if he can help us get some Kool-Aid."

Wendy held the phone to her ear and smiled broadly at Gilda's hair, struggling to suppress her laughter. "Hey, Stephen? It's Wendy! Hey, congratulations on getting into University of Michigan, by the way. That's awesome! The School of Engineering? Cool!"

Gilda sat on the edge of the bathtub. She hoped Wendy and Stephen wouldn't get into one of their long conversations about math.

"Well, I'm just here with your little sister—"

Gilda stood up. "'Little sister?!' Hello! You're not my babysitter, Wendy!"

Wendy pressed her finger to her lips, shushing Gilda. "Oh, no, we're at home—I mean, at your house—and everything's fine," Wendy continued. "She just had a little mishap in the bathroom here and we need some grape Kool-Aid ASAP."

"Give me that, please." Gilda wrenched the phone from Wendy's hand.

"Stephen?"

There was a silence on the other end.

"Stephen? Are you there?"

"Yes. I'm just leaving work. What are you guys—like, seven years old? You better not be doing something dumb that will get me into trouble."

Of course he's only worried that Mom will be mad at him, Gilda thought. "There's no problem," Gilda assured him. "We just need some Kool-Aid for a new recipe we're making."

"What kind of recipe calls for Kool-Aid?"

"The one we're making."

"Wendy said you did something in the bathroom."

"Wendy gets confused about the names for different rooms in our house."

"Don't believe her, Stephen!" Wendy shouted in the background.

"Stephen, it doesn't matter *why* we need it. Can't you just pick it up on the way home? I mean, I'm sure Mom wouldn't want me standing outside at the bus stop in the middle of the night just to go to the grocery store. She'd be pretty upset if she found out my older brother couldn't be bothered to help me finish making my award-winning Artificial Grape Surprise Soufflé recipe."

Stephen sighed. "Oh—all right. I'll get you the Kool-Aid."

An hour later, Gilda towel-dried her Kool-Aid processed and shampooed hair, which had now mellowed to a lighter shade of red-brown. "That's better," she said, eyeing her reflection in the full-length mirror in her bedroom. "Now it's kind of caramel."

"It is much better," Wendy agreed. "But I'd say it's closer to the shade of Chicken McNuggets."

"Which reminds me," said Gilda, deciding to ignore Wendy's joke, "we need to think about our Halloween costumes."

Halloween was Gilda's favorite holiday, since it involved dress-up and disguise, not to mention ghosts. She threw open her closet door and surveyed the combination of ordinary clothing, disguises, theatrical costumes, and vintage flea-market finds that made up her wardrobe. As a result of a clearance sale at a Halloween party store in Detroit, she had recently expanded her impressive collection of hats and wigs.

"Look," Gilda said, donning a wig with long, messy brunette hair. She scowled. "Who am I?"

Wendy leaned back on Gilda's bed, propping her weight on her elbows. "A witch?"

"Please. I would never be something so obvious. I'm *you*! All I need now is a shoulder bag filled with math textbooks, calendars, and staplers."

"That seems dumb," said Wendy. "I don't carry around calendars and staplers."

"It's a caricature, Wendy. The calendars and staplers symbolize your organizing tendencies."

"Fine. Then I'll be a caricature of *you*." Wendy searched in Gilda's closet until she found a feather boa and a leopard-print jacket. "Here," she said. "Mismatched weird clothes plus typewriter equals Gilda Joyce."

"Now you're just being mean. I would never wear that boa with leopard print."

"You're the one who suggested doing caricatures!"

"Well, I just changed my mind." Gilda tore off the brunette wig and tried on another option—a blond wig with sausage ringlets. "Maybe I'll be something totally different, like an old-fashioned Southern belle." Gilda put a plumed hat over the wig and stared at herself in the mirror.

Gilda's ear suddenly tickled. An image flashed in her mind: She saw an old, yellow house shadowed by tall trees. An enormous porch surrounded the house. As she looked at the house in her mind, she felt cold.

"What's wrong?" Wendy asked.

"Wendy, I think I just got a psychic signal." Gilda had spent more than a year working to develop her psychic skills. She had memorized *The Master Psychic's Handbook* by famed psychic Balthazar Frobenius, and her budding psychic abilities had already helped her solve several mysteries.

"Did you get a vision of a sheep?" Wendy joked. "Because you kind of look like Little Bo Peep right now."

"Wendy, I'm *serious*. I saw a picture in my mind—a very clear image of a house. And there was something really spooky about it."

"Was it a house around this neighborhood?"

"I don't think so." Gilda took off the hat and wig. "It kind of looked like the Southern plantation house in that old movie—*Gone with the Wind*."

"Well, that's probably because of your mom's trip to Florida, right?"

"Yes. . . . I have a strange feeling about that trip."

"You really think she's secretly visiting some guy?"

"I told you: she was giggling like crazy on the phone before she left, and her suitcase was full of new outfits."

Gilda suddenly felt sad as she looked at her closet filled with costumes, but she couldn't articulate what was wrong. It bothered her to suspect that her mother might be concealing the true purpose of her trip. She also had a premonition of some general instability—the sense that something very important in her life was suddenly out of place.

"I can't explain it yet," she said. "I've just got a bad feeling about this."

3

Darla

On a quiet street in one of the old neighborhoods of St. Augustine, a twelve-year-old girl named Darla sat on her sprawling front porch sipping sweet tea and staring at a page of her history textbook. She was supposed to be studying for a quiz on Florida history, but she couldn't concentrate on the descriptions of Spanish and French explorers in the New World. She felt sleepy as she listened to birds calling from branches in the mossy trees and the magical, sparkling sound of wind chimes as they moved in a warm breeze.

Suddenly Darla felt a presence. *I'm not alone,* she thought, sitting up straighter in her chair. She felt certain that someone was in the yard, watching her. Reluctantly, Darla raised her eyes from her book.

A woman wearing a long, white dress stood motionless under one of the towering oak trees. Her hair hung in long waves, but it did not move in the wind. She was beautiful, but oddly frozen there under the tree, and Darla did not *want* to look at her because she already knew this woman was dead.

Dropping her book, Darla abruptly jumped up from her chair and ran inside the house.

Once inside, she raced upstairs, slammed her bedroom door behind her, and immediately picked up her cell phone to call a friend. *I'll never sit out on the front porch by myself again,* Darla vowed.

It was best to keep busy and distracted—best to avoid the lonely hours during long, lazy afternoons around the house. After all, the ghosts always came looking for Darla when things got too quiet.

4

The Mysterious Gift

Gilda burst into her bedroom and immediately sat down at her typewriter.

```
Dear Dad:
    Mom has been acting weird since she came
back from her vacation.
    What do I mean by "weird"?


WAYS MOM IS ACTING STRANGE:
    Okay, it isn't exactly a shocking change
after we fixed it with the grape Kool-Aid,
but MOM DIDN'T EVEN NOTICE ANY DIFFERENCE
IN MY HAIR.
    ITEM: Stain on the white bathroom mat
from grape Kool-Aid used to adjust red hair
dye. Mom didn't even comment about it.
    No questions from Mom about what,
exactly, we did while she was gone. VERY
UNUSUAL.
```

NO SUNBURN. Whenever Mom goes to the beach, she burns and then peels like a snake shedding its skin. Actually, she and I both have this exotic trait in common. This time she only has a few extra freckles, and her skin is as white as ever. Was she hanging out with vampires? Did she even go outside??

NO SILLY SOUVENIR GIFTS!! Let's be honest: Mom has bad taste in gifts. I fully expected her to return with one of those T-shirts that says <u>My Mom went to St. Augustine, and all I got was this shirt!</u> So I was shocked (and yes, highly suspicious) when Mom gave me something genuinely beautiful--an antique crystal bracelet that's fragile, sparkly, and not like anything you'd see in a regular tourist shop. It looks like something you might find preserved in the jewelry box of a wealthy old lady who had some high-rolling times back in the olden days.

Then I noticed something else: Mom was wearing crystal earrings that perfectly matched the bracelet.

"I like your earrings," I said, thinking it was a little odd to see Mom wearing such nice jewelry.

"My earrings?" She touched her earlobe as if she had no idea they were there.

"They match this bracelet, don't they?"

"Do they?"

What was Mom's deal? Was she just pretending to be spacey to avoid answering my questions? Or had her weekend trip to Florida resulted in some kind of brain damage?

I was about to confront Mom about her odd behavior when the doorbell rang: It was a girl delivering the box of Girl Scout cookies we ordered. This was a pretty big distraction because, as you know, Thin Mints are my favorite cookie of all time.

Dad, remember that time when we drove all the way down to Disney World for a vacation, and Mom and Stephen fell asleep in the backseat, and I sat up in the front seat to keep you company as we drove through the Great Smoky Mountains, and (here's the really fun part) we ate a WHOLE BOX of Thin Mints between the two of us while Stephen and Mom were asleep? I remember how you would pretend to doze off at the wheel, and then I'd stick a cookie in your mouth to wake you up. We agreed we wouldn't tell Mom about that game. Good times!

        Okay, Dad--it looks like I have some
sleuthing to do on the home front. I'll
keep you posted!
        I still miss you, just in case you
wondered.
        Love,
        Gilda

As she read over her letter, Gilda reached for the soda she
had perched on the windowsill and accidentally knocked over
a stack of books. Reaching down to retrieve the books, she
spied something she hadn't seen in years—an oversize plastic
ring she had purchased from a gum-ball machine when she was
about ten years old. It looked like a giant, fake amethyst, and
it flipped open to reveal a game—a tiny maze containing little
metal balls. Wendy had a similar ring, and they used to hide
secret notes passed to one another during the school day inside
the rings. Gilda had assumed the ring had been lost or tossed
out years ago and, now, here it was. She felt as if she had just
received a letter sent from a simpler time when she and Wendy
had filled their days with silly games—a time when her dad was
still alive.

        Gilda put on the ring and felt slightly ridiculous as tears of
nostalgia filled her eyes.

        A moment later, she stood up very suddenly.

        Stay focused, Gilda, she reminded herself. *You have to figure
out what actually happened to Mom in Florida.*

5

Spy Report #2

ATTENTION: SPY MISSION
            SUCCESSFULLY ACCOMPLISHED!!

Dear Dad:

   As we both know, there are times when
spying is necessary for expanding knowledge
and protecting national security. True--
there are also times when snooping is simply
an invasion of privacy.

   WHAT I JUST DISCOVERED IN MOM'S ROOM
JUSTIFIES THE NEED FOR INVASIVE TACTICS.

   Here's what happened: When Mom went to
work, I tiptoed into her bedroom. I normally
have little incentive to snoop in Mom's
room because her only interesting secret
is some occasional backsliding into her
old cigarette-smoking habit. (She doesn't
buy cigarettes for herself anymore, but I
happen to know that she sometimes bums them
off the other nurses after work. Nurses

are supposed to know better, but they sure
don't always practice what they preach.)

I wasn't sure exactly what I was
searching for, but I knew I had to find
whatever Mom has been hiding about her trip
to Florida. So I put on my spy gloves (to
avoid leaving fingerprints) and I started
looking for clues.

    INTELLIGENCE-GATHERING NOTES:
General observations: a) Mom's bedroom
was messier than usual, and b) she hadn't
unpacked her luggage. (By the way, I've
noticed that Mom is very critical of my
bedroom--and Stephen's, too--but if you
ever go take a look at HER bedroom, you
realize that she's no Mary Poppins, as you
probably remember.)

I unzipped Mom's carry-on bag and found
something VERY INTERESTING--a blue velvet
jewelry box that looked elegant, but also
old and worn. Brace yourself, Dad (and I'm
sorry to be the one to break this to you):
    THERE WAS A DIAMOND RING INSIDE THE BOX.
    !!!!!!!!!!!!!!!!!!
Well, I knew right away that this wasn't
just a cocktail ring that Mom bought for
herself on a whim, or a little romantic
trinket to send a friendly message: "Hey,

25

let's have coffee sometime!" Or, "Hey, can
I sit on your couch all day while you make
my car payments?" in the tradition of Mom's
previous boyfriend. Clearly, this ring was
a marriage proposal in a box.

I was so surprised, I sat down on the
bed and just stared at that ring. No wonder
Mom has been acting so weird. I thought.
Some guy proposed to her out of the blue,
and she's probably trying to decide whether
to say yes or no!

On impulse, I decided to try on the ring.
That's when something strange happened:
Immediately, I got a very strong psychic
signal--that tickle in my ear I get when
I'm about to discover a clue to some deeper
mystery. And get this, Dad: In my mind, I saw
that same old, yellow house again--the spooky
one with the big porch. It was very clear to
me, almost like looking at a photograph.

I flipped over the box and found a label
for a place called Charlotte's Attic in St.
Augustine, Florida.

There was also a phone number, so I
decided to go ahead and dial it. I figured
that I could ask one of the employees at
Charlotte's Attic if they remembered this
ring, and anything about the guy who must
have purchased it for Mom.

I WAS NOT PREPARED FOR WHAT HAPPENED
AFTER I DIALED THE NUMBER.

The phone rang once, and a man's voice
answered in the following manner: "WELL,
HELL-O THERE, PATTY-CAKES! IS EVERYONE
EXCITED ABOUT THE BIG NEWS??"

<u>Uh-oh</u>, I thought. He must have seen
Mom's name and number on his caller ID. I
was so surprised that I actually hung up
the phone.

Of course I was mad at myself for
slamming down the receiver so quickly
and missing an opportunity to get more
information. But as I was thinking about
what to do next, the phone rang. My
stomach tied itself in a double knot:
The ID on the screen said CHARLOTTE'S
ATTIC.

I hesitated for a second, but then I
decided that I might as well answer the
call. I mean--who was this "Charlotte's
Attic" man--this strange person who refers
to my mother as "Patty-Cakes"?

ME: Hello?

MYSTERY MAN: Patty? I think we got
cut off a minute ago. I can't hear you
very well; it's a bad connection here.

ME: Um, this is actually Gilda--the
daughter of "Patty-Cakes."

MYSTERY MAN: Oh! Gilda! I've heard so much about you. Are you excited to take a trip down to St. Augustine?

ME: Sure am. (TRIP?! WHAT TRIP?!)

MYSTERY MAN: Your mom and I are going to have us a real nice ceremony right out by Matanzas Bay. Cake, champagne--the whole thing. In fact, after I leave the shop today, I'm on my way to talk to a priest friend who said he'd be willing to do the ceremony for us at short notice.

ME: (Silence. Speechless at his comment about "doing the ceremony at short notice." I'm thinking that I just can't believe it's true. There's NO WAY Mom could be planning a wedding WITHOUT EVEN TELLING US FIRST!!)

MYSTERY MAN: Your mother is a very special lady, you know that?

ME: She's certainly special.

MYSTERY MAN: When you meet THE ONE, you don't delay. No time for that.

ME: Gotta strike while the iron is hot. (What does this phrase really mean?)

MYSTERY MAN: (chuckling) I bet your mama's been showing off that ring to everybody in the neighborhood.

At this point, Dad, I felt very annoyed that I was talking to a man I had never even met about plans that, if they were real, would probably change my entire life--plans about which I knew exactly nothing. (Thank you, Dad, for noticing the lack of a dangling preposition in that last sentence.) It was impulsive of me, but I couldn't help it. I decided to give Mystery Man a piece of my mind.

ME: Actually, Charlotte--

MYSTERY MAN: Who's Charlotte? This is Eugene!

ME: I just assumed--

EUGENE: Charlotte's Attic is the name of my antiques business. But I guess your mother probably calls me Mr. Pook when she talks about me.

I barely managed to control a burst of immature giggles at the name "Mr. Pook." I wondered if Mom would actually change her name to Patty Pook, which made me come really close to losing it. (Incidentally, Dad, if I ever get married, I will definitely NOT change my name from Joyce unless my husband's name is more compelling and unforgettable for a novelist and psychic investigator. Something along the lines of "Gilda Angelista-Flashbottom" might be worth the change.)

EUGENE: Say, Gilda, why don't you put Patty-Cakes on the phone?

ME: Actually, Mr. Pook--

EUGENE: Call me Eugene.

ME: Eugene, the truth is that my mom is at work right now, and to be honest, this is the first I've heard about the "big plans." In fact, I just happened to find the ring you gave her in her bedroom. I was dusting under the radiator and there it was just lying there, so I figured I'd call the number on the box.

There was a silence at the other end of the phone that was so treacherous and loaded with significance that I actually started to feel scared.

ME: Um . . . Mr. Pook?

EUGENE (now speaking in an ominously quiet voice): I'm here.

ME: Um--I'm sorry. I was just kidding about finding the ring under the radiator.

EUGENE: (still silent)

ME (now feeling an urgent need to patch things up): The truth is that my mom wanted the wedding plans to be a big surprise for everyone, but then I kind of found out by accident.

EUGENE: (deep sigh, more silence)

ME: You won't tell her we talked on the phone about this, will you? She'll be so mad at me.

EUGENE (with an uneasy chuckle): Well, we don't want to ruin your mama's surprise, now. (This seemed to smooth things over for the moment.) I won't say nothing, Gilda. It will be our little secret for now.

I hung up the phone with a weird and not-too-pleasant feeling. I admit it: The feeling I had was something close to terror. I mean, I've been less scared in haunted houses. Why terror? I have no idea, except that something bothered me about this guy, Eugene Pook. Plus, this new development is a bit too close to home. It's one thing for Mom to have a new boyfriend--but a new fiancé? A fiancé I've never met? A fiancé who lives hundreds of miles away?

When I feel scared, it sometimes helps me to stop and write down what I know about the situation, so that's what I did.

WHAT I KNOW:

Eugene Pook, owner of Charlotte's Attic in St. Augustine, proposed to Mom, and is under the impression that she is going to marry him at a wedding ceremony on Matanzas Bay.

WHAT I DON'T KNOW:

1. Does Mom WANT to marry him? Have they
   set a wedding date?

2. If they're getting married, does that
   mean we'll move to Florida? Or will
   he move in here with us??

3. WHY AM I LEARNING ABOUT THIS BY SPY-
   ING INSTEAD OF MOM SIMPLY TELLING ME?

Well, one thing's for sure: It's time to
take off my spying gloves. Let ye olde in-
terrogation process begin.

6

It's Not Going to Happen

Gilda leaned against the kitchen counter, watching her brother, Stephen, as he prepared a bacon, lettuce, and tomato sandwich. "Did Mom tell you that she's planning to get married?"

"Is this one of your little games?"

"If you mean the 'little games' where I figure out what's going on in the *real world*, then yes."

"Okay—so who's she marrying?" He asked the question nonchalantly, wiping his mouth with a napkin as he spoke.

Gilda bristled. Ever since her older brother got accepted to the University of Michigan, he had a detached demeanor that suggested someone on his way out the door—someone whose life was about to begin *somewhere else*.

"His name is Eugene Pook."

"Ha-ha."

"I'm *serious*." Gilda opened the velvet jewelry box and showed Stephen the diamond ring inside. "I found *this* in Mom's carry-on bag."

Stephen paused, staring at the ring. "You searched through Mom's luggage?"

"I had probable cause for suspicion."

"I'm sure Mom would agree."

"Why are you focusing on my snooping when I'm telling you that MOM IS GETTING MARRIED TO A MAN WE'VE NEVER MET?!"

"Look—Mom didn't tell *me* she's getting married, so I'm not going to freak out about something that might not even be true. You don't know what that ring means. Maybe it's a friendship ring."

"Stephen, I hope for your sake that you're never dumb enough to give a girl a diamond ring and then say, 'Oh, it's just a friendship ring.' Anyway, I'm planning to confront Mom about it when she gets home from work."

"Sounds like a fun conversation that I definitely want to miss." Stephen bit into his sandwich and a slice of tomato slid onto his plate.

"I can say one thing for you, Stephen: You keep your mind on what's really important. I mean, when times get tough, we can count on you to make sure the sandwiches get eaten."

"Gotta feed the machine."

"Aren't you even a little worried about this?!"

"Nope," he said. "I'm done worrying. I'm going to college next year. What Mom does is Mom's business."

"That is so inconsiderate."

"Why 'inconsiderate'?"

"Because you're leaving me here to deal with Mr. Pook all by myself."

Stephen's demeanor softened, and he became more sympathetic. "Look. Even if you're right, consider the big picture.

It's a nice diamond ring, right? Maybe Mom actually found someone with some money for a change."

"That's so materialistic."

"It's *practical*."

"Well, if Mr. Pook makes my life miserable, be prepared to see me in Ann Arbor. I'll be standing outside your dorm room with my suitcase."

Stephen sighed. "You know what? If this actually happens and things get that bad, you are welcome to come stay with me. I mean, for a few days."

"Really?" The offer shocked Gilda. Stephen rarely even let her in his room at home, given her penchant for spying. "Thanks, Stephen."

"No problem. And you know why I'm offering? Because it's not going to happen. Everything's going to be fine."

7

The Confrontation

THE JOYCE FAMILY* APPLICATION

Applicant: Please answer the following
questions as completely and truthfully as
possible. (Watch out for trick questions!)

Date of birth:_____

Hometown:_____

Annual "disposable" income (i.e.
earnings available for use at shopping
malls, movie theaters, and costume
stores):_____

Have you ever worn, or do you ever plan to
wear, a thong bathing suit in public?

YES _____ NO _____

Do you believe in ghosts?

YES _____ NO _____

How smart do you think you are?

Genius_____

Have "street smarts"_____

Can't read the question_____

78_____

How smart do OTHER people think you are?

Smartest guy they know_____

Don't have enough friends to ask_____

My mom thinks I'm a genius_____

Why are you still single at your age?
(List reasons below and please include
embarrassing information where
applicable.)

_____

_____

_____

_____

Have you ever attempted a magic trick
that involved pulling a coin from a
child's ear? (Explain circumstances for
such behavior and how you felt about
yourself at the time.)

_____

_____

_____

_____

_____

Describe your preferred styles of corporal
punishment and the age of infancy with
which said techniques should be used for
best results:

_____

_____

_____

_____

During a family argument, you:

Take your wife or girlfriend's side _____

Take sides with the kids _____

```
Distract the entire group with a tap-
dancing routine _____


Please list any special skills or talents
you have to offer our organization.

_____

_____

_____


*The Joyce family is a registered trademark
that cannot be changed to "The Pook family"
under any circumstances.
```

Surrounded by textbooks, homework assignments, and several copies of the "The Joyce Family Application," Gilda sat at the dining table trying to study for her chemistry quiz while she waited for her mother to get home from her evening nursing shift. Her eyes stared at the Periodic Table, but her brain kept thinking about what, exactly, she would say to her mother about the engagement ring and her conversation with Mr. Pook. She was determined to tease out the whole truth.

On her right hand, Gilda wore the giant plastic ring, which she planned to use as a "conversation-starter"—something that might make her mother talk about jewelry and (with some encouragement) engagement rings.

Just as Gilda rested her head on her chemistry textbook to take a catnap, she sprung to attention at the sound of her mother bursting through the front door. She heard her mother kick off her shoes and hang up her jacket. Gilda knew her mother's routine: Like clockwork, she would spit out a wad of grape bubble gum, pour herself a glass of diet ginger ale, and take two ibuprofen tablets for her headache.

"Gilda! What are you doing up so late?" Mrs. Joyce looked stressed and weary following her shift at work.

"I'm studying for a chemistry quiz. Hey, can you believe what I found in my room? This giant sparkly *ring* I used to wear back in fifth grade. I used to pretend it was a *wedding* ring."

"That's nice, honey." Mrs. Joyce went into the kitchen.

Gilda felt disappointed; her mother had scarcely noticed the ring. She watched through the kitchen doorway as her mother took out her chewing gum and dropped it into the wastebasket.

"Mom, how do your patients feel about the grape bubble gum? It must be kind of weird having a nurse who smells like a sixth grader."

"Believe me, Gilda, there are far more noxious smells in that place than bubble gum."

Mrs. Joyce pulled a two-liter ginger ale from the refrigerator and then reached into the cabinet for her ibuprofen tablets, just as Gilda had predicted. "Gilda, I'm proud of you for studying hard, but you should get some sleep."

"It's hard to sleep when there's a *big secret* weighing on your mind, you know?"

Mrs. Joyce frowned. "What kind of secret, honey? Is there something we need to talk about?"

"Funny—I was going to ask you that very same question."

A flash of anxiety crossed Mrs. Joyce's face. "Gilda—I'm tired. What are you talking about?" She popped the ibuprofen tablets into her mouth and washed them down with a gulp of ginger ale.

"I just wondered whether there are any highlights from your Florida adventure that you'd like to share."

Mrs. Joyce pursed her lips and eyed her daughter warily, feeling, as she often did, that living with Gilda was like living with an FBI agent. "I don't follow, Gilda."

"I've heard that St. Augustine is supposed to be a very romantic city. . . . Some people even go there for their *honeymoons*."

"Okay, Gilda." Mrs. Joyce sat down at the table. "I see you've been doing some snooping, so you might as well tell me what it is you think you've discovered."

"Well, I just happened to be in your bedroom—"

"You 'happened' to be in my bedroom?"

"I was looking for a T-shirt you borrowed from me."

"What T-shirt?"

"I don't know. A T-shirt. Anyway, I accidentally happened to find a diamond ring in your bag. So I was just curious because it kind of looked like an engagement ring."

Mrs. Joyce sighed. "Gilda, you shouldn't have been looking in my suitcase without my permission. This is *not* the way I wanted you to find out."

"OMIGOD, IT'S TRUE! I KNEW IT!"

"Shush! You'll wake up Stephen."

"I hope I *do* wake him up. I should have bet him a million dollars you're engaged; then he'd owe me for life."

"Gilda, I met someone in St. Augustine. I mean—I've actually known him for a while. . . . We met online and had been exchanging e-mails for some time, and when I finally had a chance to go meet him, everything just clicked; it all happened so fast. And . . . yes. It looks like we're planning to get married."

Gilda was stunned at her mother's confession. It was the first time she had ever hoped that one of her hunches would turn out to be wrong. "But—"

"I know how you feel about new people coming into the family—"

"I've never had a problem with 'new' people, providing they've had a thorough background check. Which is definitely NOT the case here."

"Gilda, Eugene has the most lovely home in Florida, right on the water. You'll love St. Augustine; it's such an interesting city—the oldest city in the whole United States! And there are beaches and lots of haunted houses and ghost tours . . ."

"I've never cared about beaches, and—wait a minute. Did you say 'haunted houses and ghost tours'?"

"I thought it would be pretty silly," Gilda's mother continued, "but Eugene convinced me to go on one of the tours of the haunted houses, and it was quite interesting. I mean, I certainly don't believe in ghosts, but the locals in St. Augustine seem to feel that—"

"Sorry, Mom." Gilda held up her hand like a stop sign. "I think I must have misunderstood you. Are you saying that you actually WENT ON A GHOST TOUR WITHOUT ME?!"

"Honey, you're going to have lots of chances to go on the ghost tours. I know you like those spooky games."

Gilda fell silent, considering the situation in a new light. *If Eugene Pook convinced Mom to go on a ghost tour for the first time, is it possible he's not all that bad?* Gilda imagined telling her friends that she was heading down to the "beach house" for Christmas break. She imagined herself investigating ghost-infested Southern mansions and getting interviewed as a ghost-hunting expert on national television.

Still, the fact that her mother was actually planning to marry someone her kids had never met—someone she had only seen in person for a couple days—was appalling. For that, she felt her mother deserved the "Worst Mother of the Year" Award, if there were such a thing.

"Here, Mom." Gilda thrust "The Joyce Family Application" in front of her mother with the officious flourish of a trial lawyer. "I have a few questions before we move forward. You can't blame me for wanting a few details."

"Gilda, you are one of a kind." Mrs. Joyce skimmed the paper and shook her head. "You may have to cut Eugene some slack in a few areas here. Nobody's perfect."

"Translation: 'He wears a thong bathing suit with flip-flops when he goes out to dinner.'"

Mrs. Joyce laughed. "Of course not. He dresses very nicely."

"What then? You have to tell me *something* about him, Mom!"

"Okay. . . . As for why he's single: He was engaged once many years ago, but never got married. . . . And he doesn't have any children."

"What went wrong when he was engaged the first time?"

"I don't know, Gilda. He said it was a long time ago. His past is his own business."

Gilda wanted to probe this issue of his first fiancée further, but she sensed that her mother didn't want to talk about that subject. "Okay," she said. "So how did you actually meet him?"

"Well, as I mentioned, he saw my picture on that dating website I joined over the summer, and we exchanged some e-mails, but I didn't think much of it since he lives in Florida. But when Lucy won the trip, she twisted my arm to take the trip with her and meet him."

"And then he just swept you off your feet and proposed on the spot?"

"Not exactly."

Gilda tried to interpret Mrs. Joyce's inscrutable facial expression. Why was her mother being so maddeningly vague?!

"Is he like Dad?" Gilda blurted. The question seemed to dangle in midair, and her mother was obviously taken aback. *Why did I ask that?* Gilda wondered. *Would I want my new stepdad to be like Dad? Which would be worse: a stepdad who's a bit like Dad—like a cheap copy—or someone who's completely different in some way I can't stand?*

"Gilda, you know I've always told you that nobody could ever replace your dad or erase his memory. Your dad and I were high-school sweethearts—so young when we first met. We shared so many life experiences and problems together. I mean, we were best friends. . . . Eugene is different. Very *intense*."

Somehow the word "intense" didn't match the voice Gilda remembered hearing on the telephone—a man who called her mother "Patty-Cakes." On the other hand, she remembered the thick silence that had followed her fib about finding her mother's engagement ring under the radiator. *Maybe he's the jealous type,* Gilda thought.

"It's late," said Mrs. Joyce. "Let's talk about it tomorrow, okay? I'm sure Eugene will answer your questions when you see him next week."

"What do you mean, 'see him next week'?"

"Eugene told me that he was able to get the exact location and date he wanted for the wedding ceremony. It's funny, but it looks like we're getting married the day after Halloween—a sunrise wedding."

The words evoked a creepy picture in Gilda's mind: She imagined a bloodred sunrise and a wedding party dressed in witch's hats. There was her mother in her wedding dress taking the hand of a faceless shadow. Once again, Gilda felt a wave of that awful emotion—an unpleasant combination of fear and grief mixed together with a touch of rage.

For a moment, Gilda felt like crying. Instead, she swallowed her tears and stood up, determined to make her mother actually listen to her.

"Now just a red-hot minute, Mom!" It was a phrase one of Gilda's teachers at school often used, and it always seemed to get everyone's attention. "Where, exactly, are we going to be *living* after this supposed wedding on the day after Halloween? Is Mr. Pook moving in here or what?"

"We haven't figured out the details yet, but you don't have to worry. We'll stay here for the time being, and Eugene will visit when he can get away from work. At least until this school year is over. This has all happened so fast, and it will take time for me to sell the house and find a new job in Florida. Besides,

I don't want Stephen to have to switch schools right in the middle of his senior year."

"We wouldn't want to inconvenience *Stephen*."

"And you, too, Gilda. There are lots of details to sort out, and there's no need for us to rush into moving to Florida."

"So why rush into getting married?"

Mrs. Joyce sighed. "I understand you're upset about this, honey, but we're both tired now. Let's talk about this tomorrow, okay?"

As she returned her mother's perfunctory good-night hug, Gilda had a queasy sensation. *My entire life is about to be turned upside down,* she thought.

A Rude Awakening

I have an emergency," Gilda said into the phone to Wendy. She was sitting on her bed, wearing an old General Motors T-shirt that had belonged to her father. "I tried *not* to call you, but I realized this can't wait until tomorrow."

"What's wrong this time?" Wendy rubbed her eyes in the darkness of her bedroom. "You know," she said, looking at her digital clock, "I should just set my alarm for one A.M. every night, since that's your favorite time to call me."

"My mom's getting married next week," Gilda blurted.

"No way."

"Way. You know how I suspected that my mom was meeting a secret boyfriend in Florida? Well, I was right. Only it's way more serious than I thought. She just informed me that she's *getting married* to some guy I've never even met. An antiques dealer."

"Wow. I mean—is she happy?"

"I was too nauseated by the whole situation to notice."

"I guess it's kind of romantic."

"It isn't romantic! I should at least get a chance to meet this guy and decide that I can't stand him before they get engaged!"

"Gilda, you haven't liked a single person your mom has dated. If I were her, *I'd* probably dread introducing you to my fiancé, too."

"Aren't you supposed to be on my side?"

"I'm just saying."

"Well, maybe you and my mom should get together to talk about guys, since you both seem to find me so hard to deal with." Gilda watched the little metal balls rolling through the maze inside her plastic ring.

"I didn't mean it like that," said Wendy. "I mean, it is weird how fast it's happening. And I guess that means you'll have a new stepdad hanging around the house, huh?"

"Wendy—this guy has a house and a business down in *Florida*. By next school year, I might not even *live* here anymore." *Wendy has no idea how much more complicated everything is for me,* Gilda thought. *She probably can't imagine what it's like to have a family that might change shape at any moment—or to have someone you scarcely know suddenly move in with your family.* Gilda recalled the brief period when her mother's then-boyfriend Brad had moved in; it was like having a houseguest who never left, only worse. Wendy's parents, in contrast, seemed like unchanging mountains on a landscape; they were always just *there*.

Wendy fell silent, realizing that this was more serious than the usual Joyce household drama. "That's not good," she said. "I mean, going to Florida for the wedding sounds kind of cool, but you moving away—that's not good."

"My sentiments exactly. Anyway, part of the reason I called is that I just came up with a brilliant solution."

"Which is?"

"Your parents could adopt me."

"That's definitely one of the worst ideas you've ever had."

"Why? My mom could give your parents some money for the extra expenses."

"They'd never go for it. For one thing, they're already disappointed with the 'disobedient' kids they have. And they'd probably lock you in your bedroom until you got straight A's or at least straight B-pluses."

"Maybe I could focus on helpful stuff like babysitting your little brother and assisting your mom at the nail salon. See, between the *two* of us, they'd finally have the perfect daughter."

Wendy let out a derisive laugh that was more of a snort. "So how does Stephen feel about all of this?"

"He feels dumb."

"What's that supposed to mean?"

"He doesn't even know it's happening. When I tried to explain the whole situation to him, he didn't even believe me at first. Then he told me that he doesn't even care if it's true."

"Huh. By the way, I was thinking of asking Stephen to the Sadie Hawkins Dance," said Wendy, changing the subject. "Do you think he'd go with me?"

"No, I don't." Gilda felt annoyed at Wendy's nonchalant topic switch.

"Why not?"

"Because Stephen told me before that he only likes you 'as a friend.' I mean, he thinks you're smart and nice and everything, but I doubt he'll go on a date with you."

"It doesn't have to be like a big serious date. We could just hang out and have fun at the dance."

"Have you ever seen Stephen dance?"

"No."

"Exactly. By definition: *not* a fun date. And by the way, I really appreciate how you're helping me solve the problem I called you about."

Wendy sighed. "But there's nothing I can do about it!"

"I already told you my idea."

"Hey—instead of you moving in with me, how about me moving down to Florida with you and your mom? I would love to live on the beach. Omigod, think of the cute guys."

"Okay." Gilda felt a wave of sadness, knowing that this would never happen. Her life seemed to be heading in a direction completely separate from Wendy's much sooner than either of them had ever expected. "When the time comes for us to move, I'll just tell Mom, 'We're adopting Wendy Choy as part of the deal.'"

"Good plan," said Wendy.

Both girls felt a sense of foreboding as they hung up the phone.

The Journey

Dear Dad:

So it's happening. I've argued and pleaded with Mom, and I even made one last attempt to convince Wendy's parents to adopt me, but it didn't work. There's nothing I can do about it. We're going down to St. Augustine for Mom's wedding.

On the other hand, I just discovered a silver lining hidden in the storm cloud of my life: I get out of school for a few days.

"My mom's getting married," I explained to Mrs. Rabido (my history teacher), who looked very surprised and curious at first. Then she simply looked annoyed when she learned I'd be down in Florida just in time to miss the next unit test.

"You'll need to make up the work you miss," she said. (How do teachers come up with these oh-so-original responses all the time?)

"I'll make it up and then some," I said.

Why, oh why did I have to say, "and then some"? Mrs. Rabido proceeded to give me an additional "special project." I now have to keep a travel diary and report on the history of St. Augustine. "That city has so much history," she said. "I'm sure the whole class could learn something from your trip. Maybe you can even interview some of the locals."

You'd think that becoming the stepdaughter of one of the St. Augustine locals would be punishment enough. Now I have an extra school project!

I have just one thing to say (and I say it with intense sarcasm):

THANKS A LOT, MOM!!

Packing List
for the Reluctant Southern Belle:

· Fancy hat with wide brim and plume

· Historic "Southern belle" Halloween costume: nineteenth-century-style skirt with petticoats, corseted bodice, and wig with ringlets

· Makeup (because a true Southern belle wouldn't be caught dead without lipstick)

- Map of St. Augustine, Florida

- Mosquito netting for bed

- "Gator-B-Gone" perfume (ha-ha)

- Dainty Confederate flag handkerchief (just kidding)

- Investigation tools (flashlight, _Master Psychic's Handbook_)

- Guidebooks: _Florida Ghost Stories_ and _Haunted Houses of the South_

- Southern belle handbooks, including: _The Tender Magnolia: A Primer for Young Ladies of the Sunshine State_; _The Devil Is in the Details: A Handbook for the Wannabe Southern Belle_; _Becoming a Southern Belle: A Guide for the Northerner_; and _Southern Weddings_

- Ugly bridesmaid dress and dyed-to-match shoes for participation in wedding ceremony and/or use as "freaky bridesmaid" Halloween costume (with fake fangs, cobwebs, and Bride-of-Frankenstein wig)

- Tiara (why not?)

- My typewriter (because my baby comes with me when I travel)

Dear Dad:

I'm not sure why, but I feel better
after packing my suitcase for the trip down
to Florida. It's like seeing all my clothes
and costumes reminds me that I can decide
to look at this whole experience as an
adventure. Maybe it will even be material
for a new novel. No matter what happens,
I'm still Gilda Joyce: Psychic Investigator
(pen name: Gilda Angelista-Flashbottom).
No matter where I end up, I still have my
typewriter, my notebooks, and my disguises,
and I still have you to talk to, Dad. Wish
me luck in the Sunshine State!

    Love,
    Gilda

10

Wedding Planner and Spy

To: WENDY CHOY
From: GILDA JOYCE
RE: COUNTDOWN TO HALLOWEEN NUPTIALS
    IN ST. AUGUSTINE

Hey Wendy!

    I promised you hourly updates during the countdown to my mom's Halloween wedding, and I plan to deliver on my promise. (Well, at least daily updates.)

    So right now I'm sitting next to Mom on the airplane. I <u>was</u> wearing my plumed Southern belle hat, but the lady next to me asked me to take it off because she's allergic to feathers. I know you're wondering where Stephen is, what he's wearing, and what he's thinking, so I'll tell you right away that he isn't even with us. <u>Why</u>, you ask? He had to finish a special group presentation for his advanced-placement English class, so he convinced Mom to let him fly down on Halloween—just a day before the wedding. (Like I told you before, "What Stephen wants, Stephen gets.") And no, I don't think Stephen might need your help to make his morning coffee and butter his toast while his mom is out of town, so stop asking.

I thought Mom and I should use the time on the plane to educate ourselves about life in the South, so I brought a few books along, such as <u>Becoming a Southern Belle: A Guide for the Northerner</u> and <u>Southern Weddings</u>. Mom definitely needs help in both of these departments because she doesn't look or act like a Southern bride-to-be. If you can believe it, <u>she doesn't even know what she's going to wear at her own wedding!</u> <u>SHE DOESN'T EVEN KNOW HOW SHE'S GOING TO STYLE HER HAIR!!</u>

If we're going all the way down to Florida for Mom's spur-of-the-moment wedding, I'd at least like to avoid becoming the laughingstock of the St. Augustine community. Clearly, Mom needs my help with this wedding!

ME: Wearing white will be out of the question, of course.

MOM: Gilda, lots of people getting married for the second time wear a white wedding dress if they want to.

ME: But it's kind of pushing things in the case of a <u>shotgun</u> wedding like this one.

MOM: This is not a "shotgun" wedding. You really are something, Gilda. Anyway, the wedding ceremony is going to be very small and simple—just a few friends and family. Nothing fancy.

<u>MOM HAS A LOT TO LEARN ABOUT BEING A SOUTHERN BELLE.</u>

I helped Mom by creating a helpful list of all the tasks we'd need to complete in just a few days.

WEDDING TO-DO LIST FOR THE SOUTHERN BRIDE:

1. Purchase fun and elegant Maid of Honor dress for Gilda
2. Invite additional bridesmaids (suggestion #1: Wendy Choy)
3. Find tasteful bridal gown for the bride (demure, matronly style; avoid "fashion don'ts!")
4. Tie for Stephen (match Gilda's dress)
5. Prepare lengthy guest list and print invitations
6. Advertise wedding in the local paper and church bulletin
7. Order limousines or horses & carriages for wedding transportation
8. Order sky-high wedding cake with pink roses
9. Order special cake for the children of the bride
10. Order special cake for the groom (optional)
11. Plan buffet-style meal
12. Hire wedding band
13. Take dancing lessons—a must!
14. Plan and host special luncheon or tea party for bridesmaids
15. Prepare mint juleps and giant bowl of wedding punch for reception
16. Bake special homemade desserts for reception guests (Grandma McDoogle's peach pie is one option)
17. Write thank-you notes before reception ends

I showed Mom some pictures of Southern weddings from my books. I explained how "big hair is best!" and

how the bridesmaids' shoes should be dyed to match their
dresses and the color of the punch bowl. I showed her
down-home recipes for flaky biscuits, fried chicken, and
Jell-O with floating marshmallows (something I plan to
make as soon as possible).

She only laughed.

ME: Mom, you have to realize that the South is
full of these old, cherished traditions. We're coming in
as outsiders from the Motor City up north, so people
are going to be suspicious of us and our alien ways.
We might have a tough time fitting in down there. (To
be honest, Wendy, now that I've read these books, I'm
worried. What in the world will my life be like if we
actually move there for good?)

MOM: I think those books are exaggerating, Gilda. St.
Augustine has a deep local history, but it's also a college
town where people come from all over. They've actually
seen people from Michigan before.

Nevertheless, Mom said she might take me up on my offer
to be the official wedding planner, as long as I cut a few
items from the to-do list.

WHY would I want to be the wedding planner,
you ask? Because I figure this will give me a lot of
opportunities to snoop around and dig up some local
gossip about Mr. Pook! Besides, you know how I love the
theater, and let's face it—a wedding is like a big show
followed by a cast party. Of course, the bride and groom
have to stay together for the rest of their lives after

everyone else goes home to recover from the big day. (That's the serious part.)

On impulse, I asked my mom a very personal question.

ME: Can I ask you a personal question, Mom?

MOM: That depends.

ME: Do you _love_ Mr. Pook?

Wendy, remember how we watched that soap opera during the last week of summer vacation and the characters were always asking each other, "Do you love him?" or "Do you love her?" and we kept laughing because it always sounded so cheesy? Well, I now know that it _feels_ even cheesier to say it aloud, especially when the name "Mr. Pook" is in the same sentence. In fact, I think any actor who can deliver that line without bursting into laughter should be handed an Oscar.

Still, there's just ONE answer to that question that makes sense for someone who's planning to get married in a matter of days, and MY MOM DIDN'T SAY IT. (The answer is "yes," just in case you're clueless.)

Mom pressed her hands against her cheeks. She was actually blushing like a schoolgirl.

"He's a very interesting man," my mom said. "And he believes we're meant for each other."

Okay, Wendy, you better not be thinking that sounded "so romantic," or this is going to be my last letter.

STATION BREAK: Time to pause for an airplane snack of cheese sandwiches wrapped in cellophane.

To: WENDY CHOY
From: GILDA JOYCE

I'm now writing to you in secret—from the backseat of
Eugene Pook's car!! The car is very tidy, but it smells like
old wood in here.

INTRODUCING: EUGENE POOK!

Just one word: mustache. I'm not talking about a
regular old mustache; I'm talking about a very unique,
showstopping mustache with old-world personality. A
mustache that looks as if it has been pampered and
spoiled. A mustache that has been shampooed, fluffed,
and possibly even blown dry and styled with a curling
iron or tiny rollers before it was thoroughly waxed into
position. As you can tell, I was so amazed when I first
saw the mustache, I almost forgot to take in the other
details, which could be summed up as follows: older,
plump, walruslike. Definitely NOT the kind of guy you
want to see in a bikini on the beach. In short, he's no
looker, although he had made some attempt with the
old-fashioned mustache wax and a shiny new tie that
sloped over his belly.

One question: Did Eugene grow his mustache before or
after his first engagement ended? Clearly, that mustache
could have been a deal-breaker for his fiancée: "Eugene,
either your mustache goes or I go!" Maybe Eugene thought
about it for a very long time and decided to keep the
mustache. After all, he had finally figured out how to style

it. Maybe Mom is the first woman who has really liked the mustache. Or does she think she'll convince him to shave it off after they're married?

NOTE TO SELF: Ask Mom what she thinks of Eugene's mustache.

<u>FIRST MEETING:</u>
Eugene beamed at my mom when he spotted us waiting for him at the airport baggage claim. I mean, he really looked <u>entranced</u>, which made me wonder whether he and Mom see each other through what my dad used to call "beer goggles." Granted, Mom looks cute for her age, and she even had some makeup on for once. But still.

For the first time I could understand how Mom must feel: It must be nice to have someone stare at you as if they're gazing at a gorgeous painting. Especially for someone like Mom, who's always thought of herself as a "Plain Jane" (which is mostly her own fault due to her learning disabilities in the area of fashion).

"Hey, beautiful!" Mr. Pook kissed my mom on the cheek, then grabbed her hand and held it up to examine the engagement ring (which she had finally decided to wear). "It's a beauty! I love seeing that ring on you," he said.

Interesting observation: Mr. Pook did NOT try to butter me up or attempt to win me over as I suspected he might. He didn't try to act like my new stepdad. If anything, I got the feeling that he secretly wishes Mom didn't have kids at all.

He gave me a swift once-over. "Nice hat," he said. "Where did you find it?"

"My favorite vintage clothing shop in Detroit."

"Looks like a good find."

"Gilda, you and Eugene have something in common," said Mom, who was clearly eager for us to hit it off. "He has quite a collection of vintage clothing along with all those antiques in his shop."

I CAN'T BELIEVE MOM DIDN'T TELL ME ABOUT EUGENE'S VINTAGE CLOTHES! I did my best to act nonchalant, but I was pretty intrigued. As you know, I love old clothes from the 1920s and 1940s and dressing up in general, and it sounded like old Eugene actually had some fun stuff in that shop of his. As we loaded our suitcases into the car, Eugene told me all about his Charlotte's Attic antiques shop and how he spends a lot of his time appraising the value of old pieces of furniture, art, china, toys, and even old tools—kind of like the guy on that Antiques Road Show we sometimes end up watching when there's nothing else on television.

Mr. Pook is also quite the history buff, and as he gave us a driving tour of the city, he also provided a little history lesson that was way more interesting than Mrs. Rabido's worksheets.

Okay, I admit it. Despite the mustache, Mr. Pook may have a couple good points.

More info to come: I'd better start my "special homework" assignment for lovely Mrs. Rabido now.

———

To: MRS. RABIDO, HISTORY TEACHER EXTRAORDINAIRE
From: GILDA JOYCE, FAITHFUL STUDENT ORDINAIRE
RE: TRAVELOGUE ASSIGNMENT ENTRY #1:

THE ROAD TO ST. AUGUSTINE

On the road to the historic city of St. Augustine, my chauffeur drives past miles of green forest, his waxed mustache flapping gently in the wind. Here and there, I spot a few businesses through the car window—a lonely antiques shop, an auto repair shop, a funeral parlor. I must admit feeling VERY disturbed by a billboard that announces: IF YOU MOVE DOWN HERE, YOU'LL HAVE MORE FUN THAN YOUR KIDS!

Why, you ask, do I feel disturbed by this sign? Well, Mrs. Rabido, as I tried to inform you, the reason for my little trip is that my mom is getting remarried, which means that we might actually move down here. The idea that someone feels that it's a good idea to encourage parents to have more fun than their kids in Florida does not bode well for my life or for that of kids in general here. (And incidentally, Mrs. Rabido, I sincerely hope that you aren't pointing out this last paragraph to a group of cackling colleagues in the teachers' lounge.)

THE CITY OF ST. AUGUSTINE:

Mrs. Rabido, like many Northerners (or "Yanks," as the old-timers would say), you might be under the impression that the Pilgrims up in Massachusetts, with their black-and-white outfits and turkey dinners, were the first colonists ever to settle on the North American continent. Well, I'm here to tell you that you're wrong!

In fact, the Spanish landed on the Florida shore way back in 1565, led by an ambitious and puffy-sleeved conquistador named Pedro Menendez de Aviles. And when they got off the boat, what do you think those Spanish sailors did first?

"Have a snack?"

Nope.

"Give each other high fives?"

Nope.

"Write a research paper with footnotes to send back to the king in Spain?"

All wrong, Mrs. Rabido.

Really, you should know better. The very first thing they did was go to church. That's right, they set up an altar and, being good Catholics, they said the first Mass in Florida and named the settlement they had discovered St. Augustine after one of everyone's favorite saints (St. Augustine, in case you didn't realize that).

Of course, the Spanish weren't actually the "first" people in St. Augustine. The Timucua Indians were a peaceful community of farmers who had been living there for quite some time. Well, the Spanish settlers didn't waste any time doing their best to convert those Timucua to Christianity.

I'm sorry to tell you, Mrs. Rabido, that it did not end well for the Timucua tribe. Unfortunately, there aren't any more Timucua Indians left because along with church, the

Europeans brought terrible diseases, like yellow fever, that completely wiped them out.

However, it is interesting to note that the bones and artifacts of the Timucua are buried on land throughout the city and in places like the historic Tolomato Cemetery. In fact, some people believe that the bones of the Indians are one of the reasons that St. Augustine is rumored to be one of the most haunted cities in the entire United States!

Mrs. Rabido, I know you like to present yourself as a sensible lady dressed in support undergarments and low-heeled loafers, but you can't fool me. Something tells me you might share my personal belief in ghosts, _n'est pas_? Am I right?

Okay, even if you don't believe in ghosts (but I hope you do), you may be intrigued to know that the past has a strange way of _lingering_ here in St. Augustine. I can FEEL it.

Is it the aromas of traditional woodstove cooking wafting through the air from restaurants and bakeries? Is it the employees dressed in historical costumes who spend their days making candles and horseshoes to entertain tourists? Or is it simply the memories of the many families who have lived here for generations? Some of the oldest families came over with Menendez, some against their will as slaves who were sold in the old "slave market." Others are descendants of Greeks and Italians who set sail from the port of Minorca, near Spain, in the year 1768. Now considered "the Minorcans"—a label they cherish with pride—they first arrived in Florida as the indentured servants of a man named Andrew Turnbull, who

hired them to clear the land and build a settlement in a
town called New Smyrna, Florida.

Well, when they got to Florida, the Minorcans were
greeted with sweltering heat and clouds of mosquitoes thick
enough to choke cows. Hundreds of the workers fell sick
and died from malaria. To make matters worse, Andrew
Turnbull turned out to be a candidate for the "Bad Employer
of the Year" award. Eventually, the surviving Minorcans
were "freed" from Mr. Turnbull and moved to St. Augustine,
where they eventually built a vital community, known for
its shrimping and datil peppers.

GRAND FINALE CONCLUSION:
Thus, it can be seen that the past and its many ghosts continue
to lurk around in the St. Augustine community today.
THE END

I hope you've enjoyed my first travelogue entry, and that
you're coping with the school week despite the complete lack of
my scintillating personality in your classroom.
With very best wishes,
Gilda Joyce

To: GILDA JOYCE
From: GILDA JOYCE
RE: UPDATE

Now approaching the home of Eugene Pook!!

11

Darla and Mary Louise

We're getting close now," said Eugene. He drove into a quiet old neighborhood near the St. Augustine waterfront where enormous Civil War–era houses sprawled, encircled by expansive porches and balconies and shaded by trees that dripped with gloomy Spanish moss.

"Here we are!" Eugene parked in front of a large yellow house.

Stepping out of the car, Gilda felt a distinct tickle in her left ear. *It's the house I pictured in my mind when I tried on Mom's ring!* Gilda felt simultaneously proud of her psychic abilities and frightened by the implications of her premonition, remembering the cold, ominous feeling that had accompanied it.

"Eugene! Hello there!" A woman, who wore her white hair pulled back in a bun, and a girl, who appeared to be about twelve years old, approached on the sidewalk as Gilda, Mrs. Joyce, and Eugene climbed out of the car. The woman wore a long sundress with a shawl. Her willowy, feminine silhouette contrasted with the girl's rumpled Bermuda shorts, deep tan, and tousled black hair. The girl had earbuds in her ears; she was listening to music on an iPod. "We haven't seen you in quite a while," said the woman, while eyeing Gilda's plumed hat with interest.

"Well, I've been right here," said Eugene. "Mary Louise, I'd like to introduce you to my fiancée, Patricia."

Mary Louise's eyebrows flew up with surprise. "My goodness, Eugene," she exclaimed, "I didn't know you were engaged! How surprise—I mean, how *wonderful*!" Mary Louise now turned her full, inquisitive attention to Mrs. Joyce and extended her hand. "Nice to meet you, Patricia."

"Oh, and this is Patty's daughter, Gilda," Eugene added.

"Nice to meet you, too, Gilda," said Mary Louise. "We're Eugene's next-door neighbors. This is my daughter, Darla; she's in the seventh grade."

Darla looked impatient. "Mom, I'm going to be late for rehearsal."

"Darla, please say hello to Mr. Pook, and to his fiancée and Gilda."

"Hello," said Darla. She shot Gilda a quick smile.

"Hey," said Gilda.

"Nice to meet you, Darla," said Mrs. Joyce.

Something strange happened as Darla looked directly into Mrs. Joyce's eyes and shook her hand. Her brown eyes registered a spasm of confusion, as if she were about to exclaim in fright or surprise, but then stopped herself. She quickly looked away.

That was weird, Gilda thought. *You'd think Darla had just seen a ghost.*

Eugene seemed oblivious to the strange interaction between Darla and Mrs. Joyce. "How are those kids treating you over at the school these days, Mary Louise?"

"It's a mix, you know," said Mary Louise, who was an elementary school teacher. "We have some families going through difficult times."

Gilda noticed that Darla again searched Mrs. Joyce's face as if trying to gauge whether it matched some phantom in her memory.

"We're also doing a unit on the Civil Rights era, and it's awkward to bring up that pain," Mary Louise continued. "Some of the kids have parents who are still afraid of the Klan when they walk around at night; others actually have a family member who was *in* the Klan back in the days of segregation. Some of them have grandparents who wanted Martin Luther King arrested when he visited our city. In my opinion, they shouldn't be made to feel bad; I mean, it isn't the *child*'s fault their family didn't know any different back then."

"You teachers are always stirrin' up trouble," said Eugene.

It was a joke, but Gilda sensed that he was at least half serious.

"Mom, I'm going to be late," said Darla.

"If you'll excuse us, Darla has a dance rehearsal to attend. She goes to a performing arts school."

"Doesn't that sound nice, Gilda?" said Mrs. Joyce.

Gilda thought it did indeed sound nice, but her mother's transparent attempt to generate excitement about moving to Florida annoyed her.

As Darla and her mother said good-bye and turned to head down the sidewalk, Darla glanced over her shoulder at Mrs. Joyce once more, her brow furrowed with worry.

Why does she keep looking at Mom that way? Gilda wondered.

12

The Spell

Eugene led Gilda and Mrs. Joyce into a room filled with mismatched objects, ranging from grandfather clocks and rocking chairs to paintings and pottery. A spicy, pungent aroma permeated the air. Gilda felt anxious as she caught a glimpse of herself, Eugene, and her mother in an eye-shaped mirror that seemed to observe the three of them from a corner of the furniture-stuffed room.

"I use most of the space here to restore furniture and keep my extra stock," Eugene explained. "The main shop is in the antiques district of the city."

How could we move in here? Gilda wondered. *There isn't any room for people!*

"I realize it looks cluttered," Eugene said, "but everything here is cataloged. Every artifact belongs in a very specific place in the house."

Sounds like he's worried that Mom and I might mess up his collections, Gilda thought.

"Some of these pieces are actually too valuable to sell," Eugene added. "They've been in this house for generations."

As if in response to Eugene's comment, the glittery chandelier overhead flickered. The room fell dark for a moment, then the lights flashed on again.

"As you can see, the house has a few electrical problems," said Eugene. "But that's the norm for an old house in this city."

"Or it could be evidence of spirit activity," Gilda suggested. She was curious whether Eugene believed in ghosts. After all, he had taken her mother on a ghost tour.

"Plenty of people in this town would agree with you," said Eugene. "But as a wise man once told me: 'There ain't no ghost but the Holy Ghost.'"

Gilda decided to ignore this comment because she had always found talk of the "Holy Ghost" quite baffling. Didn't the existence of the "Holy Ghost" support the possibility that other, non-holy ghosts might also exist? Her eye suddenly fell on a glass-topped coffee table filled with a collage of interesting objects—spotted conch shells, sand dollars, an old silver cross, and something unusual that gave Gilda a vaguely creepy feeling—a piece of bone that looked very much like part of a human skull.

"Is that real?" she asked. The bone appeared to be a portion of a jawbone, with teeth still attached.

"Course it's real," said Eugene. "That's a jawbone."

"I mean—*whose* jaw is it?"

"It's most likely from the skull of a Timucua Indian. Someone found it ages ago when this house was first built here. It's been in this house for generations."

Gilda had an uneasy feeling. "Shouldn't a human skull bone be buried in a grave somewhere?" she asked.

"Well, sure. But this one belongs to the house."

But what if the spirit of the person to whom that bone belonged doesn't like having part of his or her head in a coffee table? Gilda mused. *After all, that bone must have been buried here before the house was built.*

Eugene disappeared into the kitchen and emerged with a silver tray of Ritz crackers topped with an unusual fluorescent-green sauce. "You have to try my datil-pepper jelly," said Eugene. "Making jelly is a hobby of mine, and this is my latest concoction."

Again, just when I think I don't like Mr. Pook, he comes up with something surprising. Who would expect a middle-aged man to spend his spare time making lurid green datil-pepper jelly? Yes, Mr. Pook, I give you points for one of the more unusual hobbies I've encountered.

"I don't think Gilda's ever had the opportunity to try datil peppers before," said Mrs. Joyce, biting into one of the crackers. "We certainly don't have them up in Michigan."

Eugene explained how the datil pepper was a traditional favorite of the region—a unique hot pepper that "goes with just about everything" and defines the local cuisine. He watched eagerly as Gilda bit into the cracker topped with datil jelly.

"It's good," said Gilda, trying not to wrinkle her nose at the odd combination of sweet and spicy flavors. *Maybe he should put the datil peppers on a pizza or in a barbecue sauce next time,* she thought.

"Patty-Cakes," said Eugene, placing a hand on Mrs. Joyce's shoulder, "you should sit down and drink some water; you look dehydrated."

He talks to Mom as if he's her parent, Gilda thought, feeling slightly annoyed with both Eugene and her mother. "Mom could probably use some maple syrup while she's at it," Gilda quipped.

Mrs. Joyce frowned, and Eugene gave Gilda a quizzical look. "Get it? Syrup for Patty-Cakes?"

"Oh. Very funny, Gilda." Mrs. Joyce leaned back into the couch pillows, and Eugene simply turned and walked into the kitchen. *I guess he's not big on jokes,* Gilda thought.

"I'll get the water for you, Patty-Cakes," said Eugene.

Gilda suddenly felt an urgent need to talk to her mother in private. She wanted to tell her about the premonition she had experienced about the house—the way she had pictured it in her mind even before coming to Florida, and the ominous feeling she had when they first walked through the door. She also wanted to complain about Eugene's mustache.

But Eugene returned to the living room carrying a glass of water before Gilda could blurt out her concerns.

"Gilda," said Eugene, "I'll take your things upstairs to your bedroom and show you where everything is in the house. I just have one rule: Please don't handle anything fragile."

Gilda felt her spirits lift at the prospect of seeing the rest of the house. With any luck, she'd have an opportunity to do some first-rate snooping.

"There are some vintage clothes up there; you're welcome to try things on as long as you're very careful."

Gilda's obvious excitement at the invitation to try on clothes must have worried Eugene because he raised a finger in warning: "Again—don't handle anything fragile, okay?"

"Got it," said Gilda. "Look with your eyes, not your hands."

"Pardon?"

Mrs. Joyce laughed. "That was a saying Nick and I used to tell the kids when they were little. Whenever we went into a store with breakable objects, Gilda was so curious she always wanted to touch everything."

Eugene didn't look amused by the anecdote.

He probably doesn't like it when Mom mentions anything about the old days when Dad was alive, Gilda thought.

Upstairs, Gilda followed Eugene down a hallway lined with antique mirrors, paintings, and furniture. She was thrilled when Eugene put her suitcase in the most feminine of the bedrooms: It had a regal-looking four-poster canopy bed, floral wallpaper, a full-length mirror, shelves displaying antique baby dolls dressed in lace, an old rocking horse, a baby buggy, and a vanity table complete with an antique silver comb and brush and some old-fashioned perfume atomizer bottles.

The moment Eugene left, Gilda felt like a young child in a toy store as she began to explore the room. She opened a trunk that resembled a treasure chest and discovered a collection of silk gloves and petticoats inside. A hand-painted jewelry box contained a long pearl necklace, clip-on earrings, and a butterfly brooch. Gilda sat down at the vanity table and tried on the necklace.

Gazing into the mirror, she spied something interesting in the room that she hadn't noticed before—a dollhouse. She turned and walked over to investigate it more closely: It was an amazingly detailed miniature world containing lamps that actually turned on and off, beds with pillows and blankets, and tiny pieces of furniture carved from real wood. The "Southern belle" doll standing on the balcony of the house had soft brown hair curled in tight ringlets. She wore a petticoat of stiff lace and a hat decorated with silk flowers. Her eyes opened and shut to reveal glass irises. She was clearly a doll meant for display rather than the sticky hands of a young child.

Next to the dollhouse, Gilda spotted two doll figurines with pitch-black faces; their eyes and mouths were gaping white circles. When she picked them up to look more closely, Gilda realized they weren't dolls. They were actually salt-and-pepper shakers. Something about their cartoonlike black faces struck Gilda as more racist than whimsical. She felt certain that many people she knew back home in Detroit would be offended by them. Did Eugene keep them because they were historically interesting relics from an era of racial segregation, or did he actually think they were cute?

Help!

It was a woman's voice. The sudden sound startled Gilda. Had it come from inside the house?

Gilda froze, listening. Her mother and Eugene were downstairs, but it didn't sound like either of them. "Hello?" Gilda called.

Help!

Gilda sucked in her breath. It was definitely a woman's voice, but it sounded strangely muffled and hollow.

Help!

"Mom?" Gilda walked into the hallway, past the mirrors

and other antiques. Was someone calling from the kitchen downstairs? Gilda had the bizarre impression that the house itself was talking.

"Mom? Eugene?" Gilda peered down the stairwell, but nobody answered.

Gilda went downstairs. Through the front window, she glimpsed Eugene heading down the front path toward his car, but her mother was not in sight.

Gilda walked to the kitchen, where she found her mother. Mrs. Joyce stood as motionless as a statue in the middle of the floor, staring out the window.

As Gilda approached her mother she felt the air around her cooling, as if she had just opened a refrigerator door. *How strange!* she thought, remembering how her *Master Psychic's Handbook* had explained that "cold spots may be signs of spirit activity."

Something wasn't right. Standing with her back turned to Gilda, Mrs. Joyce seemed transfixed by something invisible.

"Mom?"

Mrs. Joyce remained silent.

"I heard something—someone calling for help." Gilda approached, trying to see her mother's face. "Mom—are you okay?"

Now Gilda felt a tremor of fear because she saw that her mother's face looked *different*: Her mother's freckled skin had turned pale; her hazel eyes looked dark with fear. It was still her mother's face, but Gilda had the disconcerting feeling that *someone else* was staring at her through her mother's eyes.

13

A True Southern Bride

I hope you brought your umbrella, Patty-Cakes, because it's spittin' rain out there." The screen door slammed behind Eugene, who entered the house with rosy cheeks, his mustache dappled with raindrops. "Here—I found your purse in the car."

Eugene's sudden entrance seemed to shake Gilda's mother from her trance. She rubbed her hands against her temples, as if suffering from a bad headache. "Oh—thank you, Eugene."

Gilda stared at her mother. She heard Eugene rummaging through a coat closet in the next room.

"Are you okay, Mom?"

"Of course. I'm fine." She walked to the sink and turned on the faucet.

"Mom—what is your deal?!"

"Please don't talk to me with that tone of voice, Gilda."

"Mom—do you realize you were completely zoned out a minute ago?"

Mrs. Joyce rubbed her arms. "It's so cold in here!"

"You're always cold, Patty-Cakes." Eugene walked into the kitchen and placed a crocheted shawl around Mrs. Joyce's shoulders.

"Mr. Pook," Gilda ventured, "we just had a strange incident here."

Gilda noticed that her mother's eyes flashed. *She doesn't want me to say anything because she's scared,* Gilda thought. *I bet she doesn't understand what just happened any more than I do.*

"What kind of incident?" A shadow crossed Eugene's face.

"Don't worry; we didn't break anything," said Gilda hastily, "but we did hear something strange. It sounded like a voice calling for help. And I think it scared my mom—"

"I didn't hear anything," Mrs. Joyce interrupted.

"Are you sure, Mom? I heard it very clearly."

"You know," said Eugene, staring down at the floorboards, "these old houses make all kinds of noises. Why, with these old houses and the wind blowing through the palms outside when it rains, people think they hear all kinds of things— children crying, people talking, you name it." He looked at Gilda pointedly. "Of course, that explanation probably isn't as interesting as believing in ghosts."

"I didn't say it was necessarily a ghost," said Gilda, making a mental note that Eugene had independently introduced the idea of ghosts. "But I definitely heard a person's voice."

"All I know," said Mrs. Joyce, "is that I was resting there on the couch, and the next thing I knew, I was standing here in the kitchen, but I don't remember getting up to come in here. And I felt so dizzy. . . ."

"You probably just need a good night's sleep after your trip," said Eugene. "And speaking of ghosts"—Eugene grinned as if he were about to reveal a big secret—"how would you like to do some ghost hunting tonight, Gilda?"

The offer surprised Gilda. "I thought you said you don't believe in ghosts."

"I don't," he said, "but a little bird told me that ghost hunting is one of *your* favorite hobbies."

Gilda guessed it wasn't worth trying to explain to Eugene that her investigations were far more than "hobbies," and that she had already solved several mysteries, including one of national importance.

"I just ran into Mary Louise and Darla on their way back from Darla's dance class," Eugene explained. "Mary Louise invited you to go out to dinner with her and Darla, and maybe you can all go on one of the ghost tours this evening. Mary Louise—she loves those ghost tours."

Maybe he's trying to get rid of me for the evening so he can be alone with Mom, Gilda thought. She had an urge to reject the invitation, if only to thwart Eugene's plans, but the allure of a St. Augustine ghost tour was too great to pass up. *Besides,* Gilda thought, *I need to learn more about the most notorious ghosts in the city. Maybe it will help me understand what type of ghost might be haunting Eugene's house—if any.*

"So what do you say?" Eugene asked.

"Sure," said Gilda. "It sounds great."

"You can head over to her place whenever you're ready, Gilda," said Eugene. "Just be sure to take one of the umbrellas from over there in the coat closet. Now, Patty-Cakes, we need to hunker down and get ready for this wedding. For starters, you need to try on a vintage dress that I think would be perfect for you. It's cut small, so you'll have to go easy on the cake and jelly crackers until after the wedding, heh-heh. But it's a real beauty—probably one of the most valuable vintage gowns in my collection. Pure silk and real pearls."

"It sounds just lovely," said Mrs. Joyce. "And I definitely need to find a dress."

"Wait a minute, Mom," said Gilda. "I thought *I* was going to be your wedding planner." Gilda was surprised by her own disappointment. She realized she had actually been looking forward to functioning as her mother's personal stylist for the wedding, scouring the local boutiques and vintage shops for possible dresses. Of course, her mother would probably reject most of her suggestions as "too flashy" or "too silly." Still, it would have been fun to put her personal stamp on some aspect of the wedding.

"Gilda, this wedding is going to be perfect," said Eugene in a tone that made it clear that he did not want her style advice on any aspect of the ceremony. "Simple, elegant, classic. You girls don't have to lift a finger because I've already got it all figured out."

"No problem," said Gilda, doing her best to conceal how miffed she felt. "I'll just focus on things that involve the children of the bride."

"Such as?" Eugene asked.

"The children's cake."

"The 'children's cake'? I don't believe we're planning for a 'children's cake.'"

"Are you sure? I've read that in the really nice Southern weddings there's often a special cake for the kids of the bride—I mean, in these nontraditional cases when there are kids involved in the ceremony."

"Well, I've never——"

"Oh, I think that's a really nice idea," said Mrs. Joyce, who was eager to placate Gilda.

"Great," said Gilda. "I'll go down to one of the bakeries in town tomorrow. Oh, and don't worry, Eugene, because I'll ask about a special cake for the groom, too. That's another tradition——"

"We do NOT need a cake for the groom," Eugene interrupted.

"But——"

"And, Gilda honey," said Mrs. Joyce, "we'd love for you to do a reading at the ceremony. Maybe you could even write something original for us—a poem or something?" Mrs. Joyce turned to Eugene, who looked less than enthusiastic about the idea. "Gilda is a wonderful writer. And Gilda, Eugene loves poetry, just like you!"

"Perfect," said Gilda. "I'll come up with something completely *appropriate* for the occasion." She sensed that Eugene didn't trust her to come up with anything he would actually like, and she couldn't help indulging in a moment of sadistic enjoyment at his discomfort. "And don't worry, Mr. Pook," she teased, "I won't forget to order those cakes!"

Eugene didn't laugh as Gilda left the room.

I don't think Mr. Pook likes me much, Gilda thought. *Oh, well, the feeling is mutual.* She couldn't help thinking it was a little odd that Eugene was telling her mother what to wear to her own wedding. *A true Southern bride would never allow that kind of nonsense!* Gilda thought. *She'd be taking charge!*

As Gilda stepped outside and opened the vintage,

peacock-headed umbrella she had borrowed from Mr. Pook, she hesitated, wishing for the thousandth time that there were some way she could be in two places at once. If Eugene's mustache was any indication of his taste in hair and clothing, she wondered if she should hang around to see what abomination he might have in mind for her mother's wedding dress. On the other hand, the chances were good that she and Mr. Pook would get in a wedding-planning argument if she stuck around too long.

Why couldn't Mom marry someone more fun—a stepdad who would at least have a sense of humor about the "groom's cake"? Gilda wondered. *Well, one thing is for sure: Mr. Pook is nothing like Dad!*

14

The Ghostly Friend

As she made her way up the path leading to Mary Louise and Darla's house, Gilda felt as if she had stepped into a magical world. Wind chimes hanging from mossy tree branches danced in the humid breeze. For a moment, Gilda thought she glimpsed orbs of colorful spirits hovering in the cloudy air, but then she realized they were actually solid glass spheres. All around, they hung from trees or rested against potted geraniums and ferns.

"Come in, Gilda!" Mary Louise opened the door, and Gilda entered a comfortable, eclectic interior filled with the aroma of homemade cookies—a welcome contrast to the musty, spicy smell of old wood and datil peppers that pervaded Eugene's home.

"I was just searching for our umbrellas," said Mary Louise, taking Gilda's umbrella and poncho, "although the rain will most likely stop by the time we leave."

"In Florida, just wait ten minutes and the weather will change!" Gilda joked. It was a comment she had heard Eugene make several times already.

"You've got that right, honey."

Gilda followed Mary Louise into the living room. "Those glass spheres you have in your yard are interesting." She hoped that Mary Louise would explain their significance.

"I started collecting those years ago when I was much younger," Mary Louise said as she sat down on the living-room couch and poured tall glasses of iced tea from a pitcher. "At one point I was thinking of turning part of our house into a bed-and-breakfast, and I thought they would add a nice touch for the guests. It's funny," she reflected, "even after I lost interest in those crystal balls, people just kept giving them to me for some reason!"

"You were hoping to see ghosts in them, right, Mama?" said a voice from the staircase.

Gilda looked up to see Darla, who had suddenly appeared in the living room. She froze, hoping Darla would say more about seeing ghosts.

"Well, yes," said Mary Louise. "Someone did tell me that I might see a ghost or two in the crystal balls." Mary Louise's response surprised Gilda; she had expected Darla's mother to say something far more dismissive or critical about the idea of seeing ghosts anywhere. Something like, "Don't be silly!" or, "Sounds like somebody's imagination is ready for Halloween!" *Maybe the moms in St. Augustine are different from the moms in Michigan,* Gilda thought.

"But we *didn't* see any ghosts in them," Mary Louise added. "Did we, Darla?"

"No," said Darla. "We didn't."

Gilda sensed something simmering beneath the surface of this exchange between mother and daughter—some emotionally volatile story—but she couldn't imagine what it might be. She longed to blurt out a series of prying questions about ghosts in St. Augustine and Eugene's background, but she knew she had to be careful. Gilda stirred her sweet tea very quickly with her spoon. *Remember,* she told herself, *you're in the South. Mind your manners, and people will trust you more.*

"Want some sweet tea and cookies, Darla?" said Mary Louise.

"Sure." Darla walked across the living room and flopped onto a love seat across from Gilda.

"Sit up, darlin'," said Mary Louise.

"Speaking of ghosts," said Gilda, who felt too impatient to avoid the topic completely, "we actually just had a little unexplained encounter over at Eug—I mean, Mr. Pook's house this afternoon."

"Oh, did you now?" Mary Louise's eyes flashed brightly. "Tell us about it."

Gilda explained how she had heard the voice calling for help from somewhere in the house. She decided to leave out the part about her mother seeming to go into a trance, though; she found the experience troubling in a way that was just too hard to explain.

"Oh, I don't doubt that it was a ghost," said Mary Louise. "So much life and death went on in each one of these old houses. Some of them might have been used as makeshift hospitals during the Civil War."

This was interesting. Had she heard the voice of someone who had lived during the Civil War? Maybe the wife of a soldier who had died?

"Yes, I don't doubt that it was a ghost," Mary Louise repeated. "We have a ghost here in this house, too."

"Not anymore," said Darla, tersely. "He's gone now."

"Darla used to see him. She had quite a gift for seeing ghosts when she was a little girl."

"She did?!" Gilda was fascinated.

"Mom, do you have to talk about this?"

"Honey, Gilda is interested in ghosts."

Darla sighed. Her knee bounced nervously.

"Anyway," Mary Louise continued, "when Darla was younger, she used to tell me about a little 'ghostly friend' she would see in our house. She said he slept in her bed."

"No," Darla countered, "he slept on the floor in my room."

"I just assumed it was a typical imaginary friend," Darla's mother continued, "but then Darla began to tell me details about this boy's entire life." She eyed the lapful of crumbs on Darla's shorts and handed her daughter a napkin across the coffee table. "Darla said his name was Tom, and that he had been killed, and that he died in our house.

"Well, I thought this was a little strange. And Darla kept going on and on about this boy. I was beginning to worry, because she kept talking about him and by now she was getting a bit older—*too old for an imaginary friend*, I thought. So finally I decided I might as well do some research to find out whether a boy fitting her description had ever lived in this house. I went down to the historical society and looked through newspaper articles and records. And what do you know: One of the families who lived here actually *did* have a boy who was killed.

86

He was hit by a stagecoach. We think he must have died in Darla's bedroom."

Gilda observed Darla, who was busy breaking another cookie into tiny pieces. *She hates talking about this stuff,* Gilda thought. *But why?* Gilda realized that she also felt a sudden pang of jealousy toward Darla. This seventh grader had access to what seemed a veritable cornucopia of ghosts in St. Augustine, and she apparently had been born with the gift of psychic abilities without even having to try to develop them. Gilda had been working hard for years, and still she had to rely on dreams, hunches, and a healthy dose of traditional detective work rather than clear visions of ghosts to solve her mysteries. What would it be like to see and hear a ghost so clearly that he or she became an actual *friend?* And what would it be like to have a mother who took enough interest in ghost hunting to actually seek out some useful information about a haunting instead of saying that it was just a "spooky game"?

On the other hand, Gilda thought, *if Mom ever tried to help me solve a mystery, I'd probably just get annoyed with her.*

"That's an amazing story," said Gilda. "And it sounds like you have a pretty strong psychic talent, Darla."

"Not anymore," said Darla. "It kind of stopped."

This was interesting. Could you lose psychic abilities the way some people forgot entire languages when they stopped speaking them? "Any idea *why* it stopped?"

Darla shrugged. "I'm not sure."

"After I realized that Darla had actually seen a ghost," said Mary Louise, stirring her sweet tea with a long spoon, "a lot of people around here wanted to talk to her about it. In fact, one of those ghost-hunter television shows even came to our house to do a feature! It was very exciting." She paused and stared at Darla, who was brushing crumbs from her lap onto the floor. "But maybe it was all too much; Darla was a little shy—"

"I wasn't shy, Mom; I just didn't see the ghost when everyone wanted me to."

Gilda wondered whether even ghost hunting could become a chore like doing math homework once adults started pressuring you about it. *I wonder if I'd be as interested in psychic investigations if Mom started urging me to find more ghosts?* Gilda mused. *I'd like to think that I'd still be just as committed to my work, but you never know.*

"At least Darla was *honest* when she stopped seeing the ghosts," Gilda suggested. "I bet a lot of kids would have made up a big story once they had the attention of a television crew."

"I suppose that's true," said Mary Louise.

Darla crossed her legs and jiggled her foot nervously. She pulled a cell phone from her pocket and looked at it.

"Not now, Darla." Mary Louise shook her head with exasperation. "These days it's just constant! Texting on the cell phone, listening to music on her i-pot—"

"iPod, Mom," Darla corrected.

"Whatever you call it. There's always some gadget stuck to the girl's head."

"Most of the kids I know are the same way," said Gilda, who often preferred writing letters on her typewriter to sending text messages, partly because she had read somewhere that cell phones can interfere with the ability to perceive ghosts. "Some of my friends have developed radioactive halos around their heads from all their electronic devices," she joked.

Mary Louise laughed. "Oh, look," she said, glancing out the window. "The rain stopped—at least for now. Shall we get something to eat and then do some ghost hunting?"

"Sounds perfect!" said Gilda.

"Can't we just go out for ice cream?" Darla whined.

"Maybe we can do both," said Mary Louise. "Gilda is visiting from up north, Darla, and we need to be good hosts."

"We don't have to go on the tour if you'd rather not," said Gilda, secretly hoping that Mary Louise wouldn't back down.

"It's okay, Gilda," said Mary Louise. "Darla will survive. She hasn't been dragged out to one of the ghost tours in ages."

Gilda, Darla, and Mary Louise headed outside and walked in the direction of the Old City gates. As they approached the entrance to the Old City, Gilda noticed that Darla put on her headphones and sunglasses, as if trying to shield herself from things she might see or hear.

15

Gossip Girls

As Gilda, Mary Louise, and Darla walked through the Old City gates leading to the historic center of St. Augustine, Mary Louise told the story of a girl who died of yellow fever. "Her ghost still stands here by the city gates, waving to people who come into old St. Augustine. Remember when Evelyn told us about her, Darla?"

"Mmm." Darla's eyes were fixed on her cell phone; she was busily tapping out a text message.

I'm surprised she hasn't crashed into a tree or a wall yet, Gilda thought. Darla had scarcely looked up from her phone since they left the house.

"My friend Evelyn Castle runs one of the ghost-tour companies in the city," Mary Louise explained. "She's such a wonderful lady, and a true Minorcan. She's from one of the oldest St. Augustine families around."

"She probably has some great stories," said Gilda.

"Oh, she knows absolutely everything about the history of this place."

Maybe she'd be able to tell me whether Eugene's house might be haunted, Gilda thought. Eugene himself was obviously unwilling to discuss the idea, but someone whose family had been in St. Augustine for generations might know some old secrets or stories about the neighborhood.

Gilda followed Mary Louise and Darla into a bustling café on St. George Street. "There's Evelyn in the hat," said Mary Louise, waving to a middle-aged woman who wore a striking black hat with a broad brim. "Oh good, her daughter Debbie is with her, too!"

"Hi, Evelyn!" said Mary Louise, leading Gilda and Darla to their seats at Evelyn's table. "This is our friend Gilda Joyce; she's visiting from Michigan."

Evelyn was a petite, older woman dressed completely in black. Something about her reminded Gilda of a queen from a storybook. Was it the way she sat so straight, as if facing her court from a throne? Or was it her perfect manners as she delicately shook Gilda's hand?

"Lovely to meet you, Gilda," said Evelyn. "This is my daughter, Debbie." Evelyn gestured to a cute young woman whose freckles, bright-red hair, and pink Civil War–era dress with petticoats contrasted with her mother's pale, sallow appearance. "Debbie works part-time as a ghost-tour guide," said Evelyn, "but she's also a student at Flagler College."

Gilda remembered seeing a group of beautiful buildings that reminded her of a postcard from some European city. Eugene had explained that it was Flagler College—originally built as a luxury hotel for some of the fanciest rich people in the United States. Surrounded by fountains, the elegant buildings now housed college students dressed in baseball caps and flip-flops.

"What's your major at Flagler College, Debbie?" Gilda asked, wondering if there might be some kind of professional development for ghost hunters down in St. Augustine.

"Right now I'm focusing on archaeology and drama," said Debbie. "I'm leaning toward archaeology because I'm assisting one of the city archaeologists right now, and it's just so amazing seeing how all these layers of artifacts and bones are right under our feet. You keep uncovering more and more stories; it's like solving little mysteries about the people who lived here long ago."

"She digs in the dirt all morning, then she gets beautiful for the theater in the evening," said Evelyn.

"It's not digging, Mama," said Debbie. "It's excavating."

"You Castle women," said Mary Louise. "I don't know how y'all do it."

"We keep busy," said Evelyn, rather dismissively. "Oh, look, I see Tina and Captain Jack over there." Evelyn waved, catching the attention of a young woman whose style was a study in contrasts: Her romantic-looking black-lace skirt and corseted bodice were juxtaposed against a jagged, punk hairstyle, heavy black eyeliner, and a sullen expression. She was talking to a much older man who was dressed in a pirate costume complete with gold earrings, a long, scraggly beard, and colorful tattoos that decorated his muscular arms like sleeves.

As Tina and Captain Jack approached the table, Evelyn explained that the two were longtime ghost-tour guides, and that "Captain Jack Rattlebones" was actually Professor Jack Hollins—a retired University of Florida professor. "Now Captain Jack is our resident ghost pirate," Evelyn explained.

"He takes kids out on his sailboat on the Matanzas every evening and scares the daylights out of them with his stories."

"A wench from the North!" Jack joked, greeting Gilda with a chip-toothed smile. "Watch your treasure, mateys; she's got a shifty look in 'er eye."

Evelyn laughed. "If you can believe it, Jack used to be a zoology professor."

"Turtles are my specialty," said Jack. "In fact, I watched some hatchlings make their way down the beach and safely into the ocean this very morning. Aye, a sight for me sea-weary pirate eyes it was."

"Hatchlings?"

"He means the sea turtles," said Debbie. "It's almost the end of their nesting season, right, Jack?"

"Yup. From April through October, they crawl out of the ocean and lay their eggs in a sand dune. The eggs usually hatch at night, and then the turtles try to make their way to the ocean. It's an amazing sight to see, if you're lucky. Too often, they end up in some apartment parking lot or garage though, because they get confused and head toward the streetlights."

"Good thing the turtles have you to protect them," said Debbie.

"I do what I can. The other day I scared the bejesus out of a couple kids who were out there with their flashlights at midnight. They were sitting there, dropping cigarette butts into the sand and trying to start a campfire and who knows what other kind of nonsense when what do they see but a ghost pirate walking out of the ocean." Jack let out a deep belly laugh. "Oh, it was priceless. They almost fainted!"

These are my kind of people, Gilda thought, her mind brimming with questions she wanted to ask about what it was like to lead ghost tours in such a haunted city. The notion of moving down to St. Augustine suddenly seemed quite appealing.

"If you don't mind my asking," Gilda ventured, "have any of you actually seen a real ghost?"

"I've personally never seen one," said Debbie, "but I've had lots of people in my groups capture some very weird images on their cameras while we're walking through the city at night. I mean, you just can't explain some of that stuff. And I know they couldn't have doctored the photos, because I was standing right there when they took them."

The other tour guides nodded in agreement.

"I've had some kids get pinched by ghosts," Tina commented.

"I've heard that happens around the Huguenot Cemetery a lot," said Evelyn.

"It does," said Debbie. "And Tina has even had someone faint from fear at the Tolomato Cemetery during one of her tours. Of course, your tour *is* the scariest one, Tina."

"I just tell it like it is," said Tina. "If you're not up to it, stay home."

"See, Tina doesn't like kids very much," said Debbie, directing this explanation to Gilda with a wry smile.

Gilda expected Tina to either deny or laugh at this comment, but instead she readily agreed with it.

"It's true," she said. "I really don't like kids."

Gilda glanced at Darla, wondering if she was offended by this comment, but she was busy pulling apart a biscuit into about a hundred pieces, and seemed completely oblivious.

"But the funny thing is," Debbie continued, "all the kids always want to be in Tina's tour group!"

"Because they know mine will be the scariest one."

"Oh, yours is definitely the scariest," Jack joked. "Each night she starts the tour with ten kids and comes back with six or seven."

Tina grinned and shrugged. "It's up to them to keep up with me."

"If you don't mind my asking——" Gilda ventured.

"We mind," Jack joked.

"Okay," Gilda said, laughing, "even if you *do* mind, I was curious whether you guys ever feel scared while you're leading a ghost tour? I mean, it must be kind of spooky at times, walking around some of the old neighborhoods at night."

"I think we all get a little chill down our spines now and then," said Debbie.

"It's the kids that scare me," said Tina.

"You know," said Evelyn, "I can honestly say I've never been scared here. The first night I started my ghost-tour business, I put on my Minorcan dress and picked up my lantern. And as I was standing here on this coquina-stone street, I had an intense feeling that this was the very street where generations of my ancestors lived—right here in these old houses. I could really feel their spirits near me. And Debbie, you already know this about me: I definitely believe in guardian angels. I know some people might think that's silly, but that's how the spirits in St. Augustine seem to me—more like ancestor spirits or guardian angels. No, I never feel afraid here."

Gilda noticed that Darla looked up from her plate, which

by now resembled a rodent's playground filled with torn bits of napkin and buttered biscuits all mixed together.

I think Darla spent more time tearing apart her food than chewing it, Gilda thought. Nevertheless, Darla had seemed to listen very intently to Evelyn's story.

"Well, it's time for me to set sail," said Jack, standing up. "I wish you all a spooky evening."

"Tina and I had better go, too," said Debbie. "The early arrivers will start showing up for our tours in a few minutes. See you on the tour, Gilda!"

"Oh, speaking of history, Evelyn," said Mary Louise, as Debbie, Tina, and Jack departed to get ready to lead their tour groups, "Gilda's mother happens to be engaged to none other than Mr. Eugene Pook."

Evelyn's eyes grew large with surprise. "Eugene Pook is *engaged*?!"

"That's right. In fact, that's why Gilda is here; they're having the wedding this week!"

"Well, I *never* thought I'd see the day when Eugene Pook would get engaged."

"Why is it so surprising?" Gilda asked.

"Well, Eugene is just about the orneriest bachelor there ever was, that's why!"

Mary Louise laughed heartily. "You can say that again!"

Gilda felt curious. The two women seemed to share some secret memory of Eugene. "What do you mean?" she asked.

"I shouldn't say anything," said Evelyn. "I'm not one to gossip, especially with Eugene about to become your stepdad."

"Just tell me!" Gilda pleaded. "I promise I won't say anything to anyone."

"Well . . ." said Evelyn, leaning toward Mary Louise and Gilda as if about to divulge a juicy secret.

"After Darla's father and I got divorced, Evelyn tried to set me up on a date with Eugene," Mary Louise blurted.

Gilda was fascinated. *Evelyn tried to fix up Eugene with Mary Louise?!* She also hadn't realized that Darla's mother was single. *I guess having a single parent is something else Darla and I have in common,* Gilda thought.

"It didn't work out," said Evelyn. "I remember Eugene looked right at me and said, 'Evelyn, you and Mary Louise don't understand. I lost my *one true love*. Do you know what that means when you find your one true love and then lose her?' And I said to him, 'Eugene—I'm sad for you. But honey, Charlotte left you for another man. *That* isn't love.'"

"Who's Charlotte?" Gilda asked.

"Charlotte was Eugene's first fiancée," said Evelyn. "They almost got married, but Charlotte ran off the night before their wedding day."

In that case, it's a little strange that Eugene calls his antiques shop Charlotte's Attic, Gilda thought.

"Anyway," Evelyn continued, "no matter how I tried to convince him to forget about her, Eugene would just shake his head and say, 'No, Evelyn. Charlotte is the only one for me.' Oh, it just broke my heart to see him go on like that. And he used to be such a handsome man, too, bless his heart."

"He did?!" Gilda blurted. This was the most shocking piece of information yet.

"Oh, yes. Could have made someone a nice husband. Oh, I mean to say . . ." Evelyn stumbled, realizing her faux pas. "I'm sure he'll make a wonderful husband for *your mother*. I just meant that when he was younger he was even *better* looking. Over the years he filled out a bit."

"Did he have the mustache back then?" Gilda knew it was a silly question, but she couldn't resist. She had to know.

"I believe so. Yes, he always had the mustache."

"These days he's wearing it curled with mustache wax," Mary Louise added, with a smirk.

"Oh is he now?" Evelyn's facial expression made it clear that she thought this sounded like a terrible idea.

"I'd love to know more about *Charlotte*." Gilda felt as if she wanted to pinch herself to make sure she was awake. She couldn't believe her luck at meeting Evelyn Castle—a woman who not only owned a ghost-tour company, but who knew some extremely juicy information about Eugene Pook's background.

"Well, I admit I never knew Charlotte very well when she still lived here, but her family—the Furbos—they're one of the old Minorcan families that came over in the seventeen hundreds. Anyway, the Furbos are big landowners, farmers outside the Old City. From what I heard, they were so excited about the wedding they had planned for their daughter, which was supposed to be one of the big events of the year. Oh, they were just devastated when Charlotte called it off. I don't think they ever did forgive her. At least, that's what I heard. I've certainly never seen Charlotte around town visiting her folks since then."

"Do you know *why* Charlotte called off the wedding at the last minute?" Gilda asked. "I mean, aside from Eugene's mustache wax."

Evelyn chuckled. "Again, I'm not one to gossip, but from what I heard, Charlotte happened to meet a man who was on leave from the military. He was just about to be stationed overseas—somewhere in Europe. Well, she apparently just decided to take off with him. Honestly, it didn't surprise me so much. Charlotte was young to be getting married to a man Eugene's age. A bit flighty, too, from what I hear. I remember she used to help Eugene in the antiques shop when they were engaged, and she would create the strangest displays."

"Strange how?"

"Oh, she would mix things up. Once, she put beautiful old dolls in an antique coffin just to get people's attention. I guess it was artistic. But strange."

Charlotte sounds very interesting, Gilda thought.

"Anyway," Evelyn continued, "after the wedding plans fell through, I'd sometimes stop into Charlotte's Attic and Eugene would come up to me and show me a letter or two that Charlotte had written to him from Europe. It was sad how he'd just carry those letters around in his pocket and look at them from time to time.

"'You mean to tell me that Charlotte still writes to you, Eugene?' I'd ask him.'Sure, she does,' he'd say. And then he'd read me her letter about how she was traveling through this country or that country, and how she still thinks of him and misses him—even though she couldn't be bothered to show up for their wedding. Oh, it was enough to turn my stomach.

"I told him, 'Eugene, if I were you, I'd take that letter and burn it after what Charlotte did to you.'

"'You don't understand, Evelyn,' Eugene would say. 'Charlotte is my soul mate.' There was just no changing his mind." Evelyn sipped her lemonade and sighed heavily.

"Well, Gilda's mother must be one very special lady if she can convince Eugene to finally get married and forget about that Charlotte once and for all!" Mary Louise declared.

"I guess so." Gilda wasn't sure what to think. For one thing, she wasn't sure whether she should consider the story about Eugene's first "true love" reassuring or disturbing.

"I'd like to meet your mother sometime," said Evelyn. "Where are they having their wedding ceremony?"

"It's going to be down by the waterfront at the old mission," said Gilda. "November first—the morning after Halloween. You should all come!"

Gilda immediately realized she had far overstepped her very restricted responsibilities as daughter of the bride. *Eugene might not want all of them to be there,* she thought. But it was too late. Mary Louise and Evelyn's curiosity had gotten the best of them, and they were both intrigued enough to accept a casual invitation from the bride's daughter. Besides, in St. Augustine, the weddings were often big and sprawling, and the bride simply had to be willing to make room for a few more guests up until the very last minute.

"Oh, we would love to attend!" said Evelyn, "I mean, if it's okay with your mother, of course. Now, we'd best be walking toward the ghost tour; it's getting late."

"Do we *have* to do the ghost tour?" Darla moaned. "Can't we just go for ice cream now?"

"Quit whining, Darla," Mary Louise snapped. "Debbie is expecting us over there. Besides, you know you'll have fun once we get there."

Darla slumped down in her chair.

As they left the restaurant and headed toward the ghost tour, Gilda couldn't shake an odd combination of relief and revulsion as she mulled over the story of Eugene's failed relationship with Charlotte. *I suppose I should be happy to learn that he isn't a criminal or a complete womanizer,* Gilda thought. If anything, it sounded as if Eugene was loyal to a fault—at least when it came to his former relationship with Charlotte. *But what kind of person pines for years over someone who left him at the altar?* Gilda wondered. *And what is it about Mom that made him finally get over Charlotte?*

Was Eugene simply a hopeless romantic, or was there something terribly wrong with her stepfather-to-be?

16

The Girl at the Gate

Most people can't perceive ghosts with the naked eye," said Debbie. She stood at the Old City gates surrounded by a group of parents and kids who had gathered for her ghost tour. Gilda noticed that many of the kids carried flashlights and cameras; Debbie held nothing except her old-fashioned lantern. "Now, if you take pictures with your camera, you might get luckier," Debbie explained. "Some of the ghosts manifest as orbs. They're like balls of energy that look like round lights floating in the air. And if you're *really* lucky, you might see an actual face or an image of a person."

"This is where I'll leave you, ladies," Evelyn whispered to Gilda, Darla, and Mary Louise as they joined the tour group. "You'll be in good hands with Debbie. She knows the ghosts of this city even better than I do."

"Now, the first story I want to tell you takes place right here at the old entrance to the historic part of St. Augustine," Debbie continued. "A long time ago, there was a young girl who loved to stand right here and greet all the travelers who entered the city. Each day she smiled and waved to every person who passed through these gates. But then tragedy struck, and the poor girl died from yellow fever.

"Sometimes, if a person dies too young—before he or she is ready to pass on—their spirit lingers, trying to hang on to the things they did during life. Well, this young girl so missed being able to stand at the city gates watching all the travelers in their horse-drawn carriages that she just wasn't able to say good-bye.

"To this day, a lone traveler who finds himself walking home late at night after a party in town or at the beach might glance up at the city gates and be shocked to see a girl standing there, just looking at him and smiling. It's a troubling thing to see because this girl is wearing nineteenth-century clothes; she's clearly in the wrong time. She also looks deathly ill from the yellow fever that killed her. But there she is, standing in front of the gates to the Old City—just smiling and waving."

A gust of warm wind swept through the group, and Gilda felt a slight tickle in her ear. She glanced at Darla and was annoyed to see her furiously texting a message to one of her friends. *What is she writing?* Gilda wondered. She inched closer to Darla, until she was close enough to peek over Darla's shoulder and sneak a glimpse of her cell-phone screen. Gilda was surprised and a little disturbed by the content of Darla's message—a text she appeared to be typing to nobody but herself:

There are no ghosts there are no ghosts there are no ghosts. . . .

Gilda suddenly understood that Darla was scared out of her wits. *But why?* After all, Darla used to communicate with a ghost-boy every day—a spirit she had described as a "friend." Why would Darla be so afraid of a routine ghost tour through the city when she had previously experienced a haunting in her own home without feeling afraid?

"Hey! Somebody—" Darla suddenly glanced behind and then quickly moved away from the city gate. "Never mind."

"What's wrong, Darla?" Gilda asked.

"Never mind," said Darla.

"You saw something," Gilda pressed.

"I don't want to talk about it," Darla muttered.

"Follow me, everyone," said Debbie. "Next stop is the Huguenot Cemetery, where many of the victims of yellow fever were buried. In fact," she added, "some of them were buried *alive*."

"Darla!" Gilda whispered, grabbing Darla's arm, "what are you so afraid of?" By now both girls had stopped on the sidewalk, facing each other as the other kids and parents walked past them.

"I *saw* her, okay?" Darla whispered. "I saw the ghost-girl by the gate. In fact, she pulled my hair."

Gilda felt simultaneously amazed and exasperated. "Well, if you *saw* her, why didn't you *say* anything, Darla?"

"Look," said Darla, nervously glancing toward her mother, who was now standing across the street waiting for the two girls to catch up, "can't we just forget about this?"

"No, we can't," said Gilda. "Darla, why aren't you excited? This means you can see ghosts again!"

"It's not exciting." Darla looked as if she were fighting tears. "I see them everywhere, and I really wish they'd leave me alone."

17

Darla's Story

It's my mama who wants me to see ghosts," said Darla. She and Gilda walked together as Debbie led them across a drawbridge, over an old moat, and into the dark chambers and passageways of the old Spanish fort where soldiers once lived and worked. "Mama used to talk about turning our house into a bed-and-breakfast; in fact, I think she first got the idea after I started seeing that ghost-boy Tom around our place. She had noticed that ghosts seem to be good for business around here. Mama planned how we'd have séances for the guests every evening after supper—the idea being that I would entertain everyone. And of course, all the ghost-hunter television shows would come to our place to interview me. For her, the whole thing was just really fun and exciting.

"I didn't mind at first because I wasn't paying much attention to Mama's plans. I talked about my ghost-friend Tom all the time because to me, he was almost like a member of the family—someone who just happened to live in the house. I knew he wasn't alive, but he didn't scare me. It's hard to explain, but it was kind of like being friends with someone who just happened to live a long time ago. He wore funny clothes—kind of like knickers. And he said he liked being near me because I was 'warm.' He felt cold a lot of the time—a different kind of cold than you and I would feel outside in the winter, I guess. He said it was hard to explain, but he felt better when he was near me.

"He usually just wanted to play, and he said he missed having his real body because all he could do mostly was watch me. Once he told me about the accident that killed him, and how mad he was about it. I didn't know what to say. 'I guess I'd be mad about it, too, if I were you,' I told him.

"'But I'm not as bad off as some of the other spirits in this city,' Tom said. I remember he kind of warned me that there are places in some of the old houses that are kind of like portals or gateways—places where spirits can travel from what he called 'a bad place' into the world.

"Anyway, it was all fine until the television cameras showed up. Tom didn't like that. 'Tell them to go away,' he kept saying. 'Tell them to leave us alone.'

"'Why do you want them to leave?' I asked him.

"'Because they want to see me, but they don't really *care* that I'm here,' he said. 'They don't really care that I got killed and that I actually *died* here. They just want me to do something that they can put inside that box.'

"He meant television. He called it 'that box.'

"'But I can't tell them to leave,' I explained. 'My mom invited them to be here.'

"'Then pretend you can't see me,' he said.

"'But I *can* see you, Tom,' I said.

"'Just pretend that you can't. *Please*.'

"So that's what I did. They kept asking me, 'Do you see anything now? Do you hear anything yet?' And I kept saying, 'No—there's nothing.' Even though I could see Tom sitting there, right next to the cameras.

"Mama was so disappointed. They left without anything to use for the ghost-hunting show. And as you can imagine, Mama really didn't want to hear me talking about Tom after that, since I supposedly couldn't see him when the cameras were rolling. And I guess I was kind of sick of the whole thing, too. I felt so guilty about disappointing Mama, and Tom's games were beginning to seem immature. So I just started ignoring Tom—pretending that I really couldn't see him."

Darla paused and turned away from a dark barracks where Spanish soldiers used to sleep. "Well," she continued, taking a deep breath, "ignoring Tom made him angry. For a while, he acted more like a poltergeist than he ever had before—burning out lightbulbs, making dishes fall from the cupboard, stuff like that. Eventually, he stopped, and then, one day, I stopped seeing him altogether. *Maybe he just got tired and left,* I thought. What I hoped was that seeing ghosts had been kind of a childhood phase—something that I had outgrown for good.

"Then, one day—I think it was around this time of year—I was outside in the front yard by myself when something caught my eye. I looked up, and in one of Mama's crystal balls, I saw the reflection of a lady. She wore a long, white dress and was just walking through the yard. I remember having a strange feeling—kind of like a tingling through my entire body. And when I turned around, she was standing right there behind me.

"She was pretty in kind of an old-fashioned way, and she

beckoned to me, like she wanted me to follow her. I knew she was a ghost, but I was curious, so I did follow her."

Darla hesitated. She observed Debbie, who was pointing to some interesting Spanish graffiti that had been carved into the coquina-stone walls of the fort.

"What's wrong?" Gilda asked.

Darla flinched. "I'm not sure I should tell you the next part."

"You *have* to tell me the next part. Why wouldn't you?"

"Because . . . she led me into Mr. Pook's house, where you're staying."

Gilda shivered. "So tell me what happened next."

"The woman dressed in white—she just walked right through the wall, straight into Mr. Pook's house. I hesitated, but then something made me follow her. I remember the door was open, but nobody was home. His house looked kind of spooky with all those antiques he keeps everywhere. . . . Of course, I knew it was all just furniture and stuff, but still. And then I heard a voice crying, like someone was in pain."

Gilda remembered the mysterious cries for help she had heard in Mr. Pook's house. "Then what?"

"Then I saw something really weird. The woman in white had disappeared, but all around me, I saw skeletons. Some were whole, but others were just body parts: arm and leg bones, just lying around the room. Some of them were moving. Kind of *twitching*. I wanted to run, but it was like I was frozen. Finally, I turned and just ran out of the house as fast as I could. I never told anyone about it, but I told myself I would never go back inside that house. You couldn't pay me to go in there."

Gilda had to agree that this was one of the strangest and scariest ghost encounters she had heard firsthand—and she had witnessed some pretty terrifying things. "What do you think it meant?" she asked, doing her best to maintain the objective attitude of an investigator as she and Darla followed the tour group back through the fort and up a steep walkway leading to the old cannons.

"I'm not sure, but one time I heard Mrs. Castle saying that some of the houses in our neighborhood were used as makeshift hospitals during the Civil War. She said the bullets back in the Civil War days shattered the entire bone if you got hit, so they ended up having to amputate a lot of arms and legs without any anesthesia. Who knows, maybe all that pain from soldiers left some kind of imprint on the house or something."

"It's possible," said Gilda. "We should do some more research so we can find out for sure. We should try to figure out who that woman in white is, too."

"I'm not doing any research on ghosts. No way."

"Why not?"

"I don't want to see ghosts anymore."

"Fine, but it sounds like you're going to keep seeing ghosts whether you want to or not."

"When I'm on the phone or listening to music I usually don't see them, and I just try to avoid looking around too much."

"You could also get one of those plastic ghost-proof bubbles to live inside. We'll just send you your meals through a little flap and roll you down the sidewalk on wheels."

Darla stared at Gilda, perplexed.

"I was joking!"

"Oh. Because it kind of sounded like a good idea."

"Darla, you won't be able to avoid ghosts forever, especially living in this city. And the truth is, avoiding them is a waste of your talent. You just have to learn how to handle your gift."

"I don't feel talented," said Darla. "I feel weird."

"But you *are* talented. In fact, you remind me a little bit of my mentor, Balthazar Frobenius. He started seeing ghosts and a lot of other things when he was just a kid, and he didn't want to at first either. But it turned out he couldn't ignore it; he finally realized he had to train himself to use his abilities in some positive way. He's had an amazing career."

"I suppose you and Mama would be thrilled if I became a psychic or a ghost hunter or whatever, but that's not what I want. I just want to be a normal kid!"

Gilda felt frustrated. *I wonder if there's some way Darla and I could switch parents,* she thought. *I could start a bed-and-breakfast with Mary Louise and Darla could play video games with Stephen.* On the other hand, Gilda realized that switching parents would mean that Darla would have to stay at Eugene's house, and she'd be way too frightened to handle that. *I may not have Darla's natural talent for perceiving ghosts,* Gilda reflected, *but at least I'm brave enough to face them. What's the use of being talented if you're too scared to actually develop your gifts?*

"Darla," said Gilda, "you simply *aren't* a normal kid, and you're going to have to accept that."

Darla stared out at the starlit sky and the black water of the Matanzas Bay. Tears welled in her eyes, and Gilda immediately regretted the statement. "Look, I didn't mean it like something *bad*. I just mean that you're special."

"Look, I just want to go home," Darla said with a sniff. "Please—don't talk to me about ghosts anymore, okay?"

Darla walked briskly away, leaving Gilda behind. Gilda started to chase after her, but then decided to let her walk ahead; she was clearly trying to put as much distance as possible between herself and the ghost-tour group.

18

Gilda's Ghost Tour

TO: WENDY CHOY
FROM: GILDA JOYCE
RE: St. Augustine ghost-hunting update

Dear Wendy:
One thing's for sure: Ghosts are drawn to
St. Augustine like moths to a cashmere
sweater in the back of an old lady's
closet. They're <u>everywhere.</u> I've <u>already</u>
had my first unexplained encounter at Mr.
Pook's house (strange voice calling for
help; source not yet identified). Not only
that, the girl who lives next door has
amazing psychic abilities. (Unfortunately,
she's a bit of a wuss when it comes to
actually facing real ghosts.)

NEWS FLASH: <u>MAJOR DISCOVERY ABOUT MR.</u>
<u>EUGENE POOK!</u>

I just discovered that a long time ago,
Mr. Pook was engaged to a woman named
Charlotte Furbo, who wisely left him for
another man. Apparently, Eugene never got
over Charlotte until he met my mom.

What can I say, Wendy? Life is very
strange.

On a positive note, St. Augustine has
not failed to provide a healthy dose of
intrigue.

MYSTERIES IN PROGRESS:

What was the source of the cries for help
I heard in Eugene Pook's house when Mom
and I first arrived? Is the voice connected
with Darla's story about seeing skeletons
and severed limbs in this house? Is there
some link with traumatic events that
happened way back during the Civil War
and who is the ghostly woman in white?
What was she trying to tell Darla about
Mr. Pook's house?

HOW CAN I HELP DARLA?

I feel bad for her; it can't be easy to
be scared literally all the time. How can
I convince Darla to get over her fears

so she can help me do some ghost hunting?
Yes, Wendy, there is a selfish motive here.
At the same time, I really do want to
help. So far, I helpfully told her that
she's "not normal," which resulted in
tears. (NO INSULTS ABOUT MY LACK OF TACT,
PLEASE.)

More to come: I need to pause to write
my travelogue for Mrs. Rabido before she
goes into withdrawal as a result of my
absence from her class.

TO: MRS. RABIDO
FROM: GILDA JOYCE
RE: ST. AUGUSTINE TRAVELOGUE Entry #2

Dear Mrs. Rabido:
You might be interested to know that I'm
writing to you from a haunted house. Now,
you might think this isn't a big deal,
since most of the houses in the old part
of St. Augustine are at least a little bit
haunted, but let me assure you, it is still
quite scary.

Just so you can picture me: I'm sitting
up in an old-fashioned bed complete with
a feather-stuffed mattress and hand-sewn
quilts. I'm trying not to look around the
room too much, because the faces of about a

hundred antique dolls look kind of freaky
in the dim light. Listen! The click, clack,
clack of my typewriter is punctuated by
bursts of thunder and flashes of lightning
from outside. Indeed, Mrs. Rabido, here in
St. Augustine it is literally "a dark and
stormy night."

If I'm lucky, both this homework
submission and I will reach you in good
health, allowing you to carefully print
the letter A with a steady hand, using
your lovely red pen. Let's keep our fingers
crossed, Mrs. Rabido!

Since I know you love excitement, I've
arranged a special treat for you tonight.
Get ready, Mrs. Rabido: Strap yourself into
your corset and bonnet, and grab a few
extra batteries for your flashlight. We're
heading out for GILDA'S GHOST TOUR OF YE
OLDE CITY!

Our first stop--the lovely Huguenot
Cemetery, which is filled with mossy,
teetering tombstones. This cemetery "opened
for business" in the year 1821 as a final
resting place for "non-Catholics," partly
because there was nowhere else to bury all
the people who died during an epidemic of
yellow fever. What is yellow fever, you
ask? Let's just say that if you got the

yellow fever, you would have been lucky if you died <u>right</u> <u>away</u>. (Notice that this was the "lucky" outcome, Mrs. Rubido.)

If you were NOT lucky, you went into a coma. And all too often, that meant that you were hastily stuffed into a coffin and enthusiastically buried by the overzealous townsfolk, who might have overlooked one teeny, tiny detail.

OOPS! YOU WERE STILL ALIVE!!

"We know that A LOT of people were buried alive by accident," Debbie Castle, a local ghost-tour guide and student archaeologist, cheerfully explained during tonight's ghost tour. "They've found the scratch marks on the insides of coffins when they are exhumed."

But if you were rich, Mrs. Rabido, then you might be able to afford being buried a very special way. A string would be tied to your finger—a very long string that would also be attached to a little bell ABOVEGROUND at the other end. That way, if you just happened to have the nasty surprise of waking up to find yourself inside a coffin, you could let someone aboveground know about the terrible mistake before it was TOO LATE.

Of course, this service wouldn't come

cheap, Mrs. Rabido, so don't go expecting anyone to do it for free. You had to <u>pay</u> someone to hang out near your tombstone around the clock--hopefully someone who would stay there without taking too many long bathroom breaks; someone who would remember to <u>listen</u> for that bell! And let's be frank--hopefully someone who received good grades from you in history class! Let us hope that you choose the right person, Mrs. Rabido, should you ever find yourself in such an unfortunate position.

<u>GHOSTS OF THE OLD FORT</u>:
Next, Mrs. Rabido (if you're still conscious and haven't passed out from fright), I will lead you down to the Castillo de San Marcos (also known as "The Old Fort").

In the darkness, with only our flashlights and the moon shining down on the dark water of the bay, we can imagine a time back in the 1600s, when the Spanish soldiers paced back and forth during the night, keeping watch over the horizon and prepared to launch their cannons at any moment if they fell under attack.

Follow me across a drawbridge suspended

over a murky moat where alligators used to
lurk. Inside the fort we go, down the steps
and into the living quarters. Notice the
old communal latrine where soldiers went
to poop. Here, the ghosts of smells past
sometimes waft through the air.

Now we see a row of sleeping quarters
where the walls are smudged with the
graffiti and carvings of bored, homesick
Spanish soldiers.

There are many ghost stories from the
old fort, Mrs. Rabido, so I'll share one of
the local favorites:

PRISONERS OF LOVE
Once upon a time, some archaeologists were
doing an excavation of one of the rooms
in the old fort, and they found bones.
People speculated about the bones: Had they
discovered an old dungeon in the old fort?
Maybe a torture chamber?

Well, eventually someone came forward
to tell the tragic tale of a jealous
Spanish colonel whose young wife fell in
love with another officer in the Spanish
army. When the colonel discovered the
affair, he decided to punish his wife by
giving her exactly what she wanted--the
opportunity to be with her lover forever.

The Spanish colonel ordered his men to
chain the two lovers together and seal
them into an airtight room where they
would gradually suffocate and die in each
other's arms.

(Sorry Mrs. Rabido; I warned you that
this was a scary story!)

But here's good news: Now you can
breathe a sigh of relief, Mrs. Rabido. As
it turned out, this story is about as true
as the headlines in our school newspaper.
That's right; the story is completely made
up--a local legend. The truth was that the
archaeologist had discovered animal bones
in the fort's old trash room. Of course,
that's not as exciting as lovers sealed in
a dungeon, is it?

Gilda looked up from her typing and caught a glimpse of herself in the full-length mirror affixed to the wall. She looked small and vulnerable, crouching in front of her typewriter, which she had propped up on a stack of leather photo albums and an embroidered pillow. A gauzy canopy curtain was draped around her bed, reminding her of a little tent. Gilda remembered how, when she was younger, she had wanted a "princess bed" like this one. But in Eugene's house, the bed was spookier than she had expected: The shadows of objects glimpsed through the filmy curtain had an eerie, animated quality. Every now and then, she had the distinct feeling that something in the room was silently *moving* around her.

Outside, Gilda heard the whistling of wind in the trees followed by a rumble of thunder. A bright flash of lightning illuminated a row of staring glass eyes—the vintage dolls.

Gilda ducked under her covers and squeezed her eyes shut. It was a perfect night for ghost hunting, but she suddenly felt frightened and overwhelmed, as if all the ghosts in the city had followed her home after the ghost tour. She pictured them drifting toward Eugene's house, peering in the windows and slipping under doorways, wanting to speak to her. She suddenly felt even more sympathy for Darla, who must feel this way most of the time. *No wonder she keeps her eyes on her cell phone as much as possible,* Gilda thought. *For her, every day must be like looking around a strange bedroom in the middle of the night.*

Gilda opened her suitcase and took out a small pewter crucifix that had once belonged to her grandmother McDoogle. She remembered her grandmother telling her that the object had been a gift from her own mother, and that it had special "protective powers."

Holding the smooth cross in her hand and curling up under the covers, Gilda reminded herself of the advice she heard Debbie give to kids who got scared on the ghost tours: "Just tell the ghosts, 'Go away!'"

"Go away," Gilda whispered as she tried to will herself to fall asleep.

19

The Woman in White

Gilda awoke to the clanging sound of an antique bell.

"Get up," someone said. "You fell asleep on the job."

The bell rang louder, and Gilda realized that she had fallen asleep in the middle of the Huguenot Cemetery.

"She'll die if you don't hurry."

I need to find her grave, Gilda thought. But as she walked, she realized she didn't know whose grave to look for. As she hurried past tombstones, heavy pieces of furniture moved in front of her to block her path: grandfather clocks, wooden benches, mirrors, leather-bound photograph albums, tall stacks of china dishes, giant baby dolls wearing elaborate petticoats, "black Americana" knickknacks.

A sickly sensation moved through Gilda's body. She knew someone had been buried alive by accident, but whom? How could she know which of the graves contained the person calling for help?

"I need a shovel!" Gilda called. "Someone's calling for help down there!"

Across the cemetery, a row of shadowy strangers observed her silently, but made no move to help.

"You're trespassing!" one of them called to her. "Get off the property."

"There's no time left! We have to help her!" Gilda dropped to her knees and tried to dig into the ground with her bare hands, but the dirt turned into hard wood; her efforts were futile. The final moment passed, and the bell fell silent.

She sat alone with the cold tombstones, the quiet bones, and the ghost-woman who glided through the cemetery wearing a gown of white silk.

20

The Message in the Dollhouse

Gilda awoke with a feeling of relief to find herself safe in bed and not outside digging in a cemetery. Had the ghost tour caused her nightmare? Or was it something about Eugene's house that filled her dreams with cemeteries and ghosts?

Gilda stared up at the grandfather clock, listening to its eerily soothing ticking and the creaking of footsteps coming from somewhere in the house. She jumped to her feet, pulled on a pair of jeans and a T-shirt, and tiptoed into the hallway. As her eyes adjusted to the dim morning light, she surveyed the objects arranged and stacked outside her door and realized something looked different. Hadn't the dollhouse been in her room when she first went to bed? Now, inexplicably, it was outside in the hallway. Looking more closely, Gilda saw something even more puzzling: A pair of very tiny shoes and the lace hem of a dress peeked out from beneath the toy house. Someone had purposefully placed one of the Southern belle dolls beneath the dollhouse to make it look as if the doll were being crushed. Inside the dollhouse, tiny tables, chairs, dishes, and paintings were turned over and tossed in a jumble, as if a bunch of mice had snuck into the little rooms and thrown a destructive party.

Had Eugene or her mother moved the dollhouse during the night? Or was this evidence of a poltergeist in Mr. Pook's house?

Eugene emerged from his bedroom wearing an old-fashioned pair of pajamas with red stripes. He rubbed the top of his balding head, squinting without his glasses. Gilda stifled a laugh: At the moment, he reminded her of a rotund, grumpy Christmas elf with one tip of his mustache pointing skyward and the other sticking straight out.

"Morning," said Gilda. She observed him closely, watching for clues.

"Oh—good morning. Sleep okay through that storm?"

"I had a really weird dream." Gilda couldn't quite remember the dream, but there had been something about digging in the ground. The dream had left her with the unpleasant feeling that an important task remained unfinished.

Eugene put on his glasses and suddenly noticed the dollhouse in the hallway. He frowned as he took in the scene— the little shoes and tiny petticoat of the Southern belle doll protruding from beneath the house.

"Why is this dollhouse out here in the hallway?" Eugene spoke quietly, but Gilda sensed his rising blood pressure.

"I have no idea." Gilda did her best to hold her ground and look Eugene straight in the eye. "I was just going to ask you the same question."

"I didn't move it."

"Neither did I."

He obviously didn't believe her. *If Eugene didn't move it,* Gilda thought, *then this must be more evidence of a haunting.*

Gilda attempted to lighten the mood: "Remember the old *Wizard of Oz* movie? That doll's feet sticking out from under the house reminds me of the scene where Dorothy's house falls down on top of the witch."

Ignoring Gilda's anecdote, Eugene wordlessly walked over to the dollhouse, hoisted it up, and removed the doll. He adjusted her dress and gently placed her back inside the house. "This is a very expensive item," said Eugene, his lopsided mustache dancing above his lip as he spoke. "And I specifically asked you not to move any of these objects."

"I know," said Gilda. "And I *didn't.*" *If he's this mad about an object being moved, what would he do if something actually broke?* "Maybe my mom knows something about it," Gilda added, although moving a dollhouse in the middle of the night didn't sound like something her mother would do.

"Your mother's mad at me," Eugene said, sighing.

"Really?" This comment surprised and intrigued Gilda. "Why?"

"Turns out we see a few things differently."

Is this about the mustache? Gilda wondered.

"It's about wedding flowers." He stared at the dollhouse glumly.

"What *about* them?" *Eugene sure doesn't waste words,* Gilda thought. Getting him to actually explain something seemed to take a ridiculous amount of effort.

"We need to have white lilies at the ceremony, but she wants pink roses."

Why does he care what kind of flowers they have? Gilda wondered. *And does he expect me to take his side against my mom?*

"I guess when you spend time in the antiques business you get some very particular ideas," Eugene continued. "I *know* the lilies will look much better with the lines of her dress, but she doesn't believe me."

"I could take a look at both types of flowers and give you my expert opinion," Gilda suggested. "That's the kind of service I'd offer as your wedding planner."

Eugene chuckled, but he also turned away from Gilda quickly, as if to show her that he hated this idea. "That's okay," he said, "we'll figure it out. Anyway, your mother wanted me to tell you that we're having a wedding rehearsal down by the waterfront at eleven this morning."

"We're having the rehearsal this morning?! But Stephen isn't even here."

"It's the only time we could find when the priest and the musicians could meet with us at such short notice. We just want to make sure we're all on the same page."

"Okay," she said, "but what about my reading? I haven't even written my wedding tribute poem yet."

"Don't worry about that; the priest can give you a verse to read."

Gilda was not about to let the priest pick out a verse when she herself had an opportunity to select—or better yet, write—a truly unique reading for the wedding. After all, she loved any opportunity for a performance, and her mother's wedding was no exception.

Gilda glanced at the clock and sighed. *I'd better get busy,* she told herself, reluctantly turning her attention away from the mystery of the moving dollhouse. *I need to figure out what I'm wearing to the wedding and come up with a wedding poem by 11:00 this morning. But how am I supposed to concentrate on wedding plans when an actual poltergeist is on the scene?!*

21

The Ghost in the Mist

Gilda dashed into the guest bedroom and opened her suitcase. She was tempted to wear her "freaky bridesmaid" costume to the wedding rehearsal as a joke, but decided it would be best to save it for Halloween.

Instead, she pulled open the swinging doors of an antique armoire, where vintage dresses hung in a row. Gilda loved trying on old, formal clothes that suggested a more elegant, theatrical time, and these dresses looked particularly fun. She selected a sleeveless dress made of pale, sea green silk and slipped it over her head. The 1920s-style gown was long, loose, and flowing, with a drop waist. She pulled open one of the drawers where she found a pair of long gloves decorated with tiny white pearl buttons and a beaded clutch purse that sparkled as if it were covered with jewels. The final touch was a vintage hat tied with a velvet ribbon.

Gilda smiled when she saw her reflection in the mirror. *It's perfect for the wedding,* she thought: *vintage, simple, and elegant.* With any luck, Eugene would let her wear it. *But if only I could wear this dress to an elegant party or ball instead of Mom's wedding!* Gilda contemplated styling her hair in an updo, but when she glanced at the grandfather clock, she realized she had better head out and find a good spot to work on her wedding poem.

Gilda cracked open the window to check the weather and a humid breeze filled the room with the scent of rain. Looking outside, Gilda suddenly had a tingly feeling that was similar to the tickle she often felt in her left ear when picking up a psychic vibration. But this feeling was more intense: It permeated her entire body. What Gilda saw out the window made her feel as if she had momentarily stepped into a magical dimension: An eerily beautiful woman whose dark hair and ivory silk gown rippled in the breeze walked through the early-morning mist, her bare, white feet padding over the wet ground. Gilda froze for a moment, just staring at the vision.

Somehow she knew that this woman was not alive. *I'm seeing a ghost,* Gilda told herself. *And in my experience, ghosts tend to surface when there's an urgent problem to be solved.*

There wasn't time to change back into her regular clothes. In Gilda's experience, ghosts only surfaced if they had something urgent to communicate. She hurriedly slipped on her shoes, grabbed her notebook and backpack, and ran from the room to follow the ghost.

22

The Truthful Letter

Outside, Gilda was surprised to spy a crab crawling through a puddle right in the middle of Water Street. The storm had left the sidewalks and streets messy with mossy branches and palm fronds that had fallen during the night. Even bits of ocean life had blown into people's yards, far from the beach. There was, however, no sign of the woman in white; she had vanished.

Who is she? Gilda wondered. The woman had looked completely solid, but Gilda remembered the unique, tingling sensation she had experienced—the distinct feeling that she was seeing a ghost. *I wonder if it's the same ghost that Darla saw,* Gilda thought, *the woman in white.*

Gilda suddenly felt annoyed that she couldn't run straight over to Darla's house, knock on the door, and blurt out everything she had just seen. *Here I am,* Gilda thought, *staying in a haunted house—right next door to a girl who has even better psychic powers than I do . . . and she refuses to talk to me about ghosts!*

Gilda took one last look down the street, but decided to give up looking for clues when she felt her stomach rumbling. It wasn't likely she was going to do very good detective work on an empty stomach. She glanced at her watch and figured she had just enough time to grab some breakfast in the Old City, scribble down a quick but awe-inspiring wedding poem, and then head down to the waterfront for the wedding rehearsal.

Gilda walked down St. George Street and decided to investigate a small, rustic building called the Spanish Bakery. Inside, a woman wearing a traditional corseted dress and apron lifted a tray of empanadas from an old woodstove. The aroma of fresh bread, pastries, and meat pies filled the air.

"Those smell amazing," said Gilda, eyeing the empanadas.

"Spanish meat pies," said the woman. "Good choice."

Gilda reflected that it would be convenient if more foods were available in pie form for on-the-go consumption. She made a mental note to share that idea with Mrs. Rabido in her next travelogue entry, since she had spied Pop-Tarts in her teacher's desk drawer on more than one occasion. As Gilda paid for her empanada, she noticed a tray of small pastries shaped like little skulls with bones attached.

"What are those?" Gilda asked, pointing.

"Those are *Huesos de Santo*: 'Bones of the Holy' in Spanish. In Spain they sometimes make them especially for Halloween. Here: This one broke; you can try it for free."

Gilda bit into the pastry, which tasted faintly of licorice.

"We make a special dough with anise seed and an orange glaze and then shape it into a skull with bones attached," the woman explained. "I grew up in Spain, and when I was a little girl, sometimes we'd go put some of these on the graves of our dead relatives on Halloween night. For this one night, the living and the dead are reunited—breaking bread together."

Gilda loved this idea and decided to buy a bag of "Bones of the Holy" pastries with the idea of taking some back to Michigan to place on her father's grave. *Although,* she thought, *if he were still alive he would probably say that giving food to dead people sounds like a ridiculous idea.*

With her empanada and "Bones of the Holy" pastries in hand, Gilda sat down at one of the picnic tables outside the bakery. She opened her notebook, pulled a pen from her backpack, and sat, poised to receive inspiration to write a splendid wedding poem.

Gilda rarely suffered from writer's block, so it was unusual that she couldn't think of a single thing to say on the occasion of her mother's wedding. *At least not anything that Mom and Eugene would* want *to hear on their wedding day,* she thought. *But maybe I'm stuck because I'm trying too hard to please them.*

Gilda decided to get started by writing a totally honest letter instead:

Dear Eugene and Mom:

Do you want to know the truth? I wish this wasn't even happening. The truth is, Mr. Pook, that I don't like you very much. I don't even like your mustache.

There, I said it. In fact, if I could get away with it, I would tiptoe into your bedroom during the night, shave off half of your mustache, then freak you out by leaving a ransom note from the kidnapped mustache.

Pretty mean, huh?

I know; you don't have to say it. You don't like me much either. I get that, okay?

But here's the problem: I don't mean to gross you out, but if you haven't noticed, WE'RE ACTUALLY GOING TO BE STUCK TOGETHER IN THE SAME FAMILY!!!

Maybe eventually, we'll find some common ground. For example, we both like vintage clothes (you like storing them; I like wearing them), and we both like cooking (you like making datil-pepper jelly; I like making peanut butter, banana, and chocolate sandwiches). Perhaps these are starting points, Mr. Pook. But until we find something to like about each other, I guess we'll just have to "agree to disagree," "let sleeping dogs lie," and other peacekeeping clichés.

And Mom, I do want you to be happy. Even though I personally am not happy, I promise to "sacrifice myself to the table" as they say in prowrestling and will do my best to give Mr. Pook a chance.

With begrudging tolerance on your special day,
Gilda

Gilda felt a little better after putting her honest feelings down on paper. Still, time was dwindling, and she knew she had to come up with something that she could actually read in public at the wedding.

As she sat doodling on her paper, she watched an old man dressed in a colonial Spanish costume with ruffled sleeves read his newspaper at one of the nearby tables. His wife sat down across from him, dressed in ordinary shorts and a T-shirt. The two smiled at each other as they munched on a plate of Bones of the Holy pastries.

I wonder if Mom and Eugene will ever be like those two in their old age, Gilda mused. Would they still be together? For some reason, Gilda couldn't picture it, but the notion of an aging couple seeking companionship inspired her to scribble some verses. She spent the next few minutes quickly writing a draft of her wedding poem:

"THE HOUR OF EARTHLY NEED!"
A wedding poem by Gilda Joyce

It brings a tear of joy,
'Tis a sweet thing indeed!
When two older folks
In their hour of earthly need;

Can turn to each other
And stand hand in hand;
No feeble-brained woman!
No plump-bellied man!

Just a fab North-South duo—
(Let's hope they're a team!)
The St. Augustine King
And his Michigan Queen!

Gilda wasn't completely satisfied with the poem, which struck her as a tad insincere. *It will have to do for now,* she thought. With a deep sigh of resignation, Gilda stashed her notebook into her backpack and headed toward the waterfront for the wedding rehearsal.

23

The Secret Invitation

As she approached the Mission of Nombre de Dios on the waterfront, Gilda made her way down a curving, shaded path marked with small monuments devoted to the seven sorrows of the Virgin Mary—mounds of engraved stones topped with . crosses. When she reached the rustic altar that marked the site of the first Catholic Mass on North American soil, Gilda looked around for evidence of the wedding rehearsal but found that she was the first person to arrive.

The day had suddenly turned gloomy, and a fine layer of mist now lay over the Matanzas Bay. As a small sailboat drifted toward the shore, Gilda watched a man who looked, from a distance, like a seafarer from an earlier time in history drop anchor and wade onto the shore.

As Gilda drew closer, she recognized Captain Jack's head scarf, gold earrings, tattoos, and scraggly beard. *What is he doing here?* Gilda wondered, observing the "ghost pirate" she had met the night before. He seemed to be looking for something on the ground. *If I didn't know better, I would think I'm seeing the ghost of a real pirate searching for his buried treasure,* Gilda thought, watching him with interest.

"Hey! Captain Jack!"

Captain Jack squinted at Gilda, not recognizing her at first in the long, vintage dress and hat she wore. "It's me—Gilda Joyce!"

Jack raised a hand in a greeting, but he put his finger to his lips, indicating that he didn't want to make any noise. He pointed at something on the ground.

"That's a gopher," he whispered as Gilda approached him.

"A gopher?" Gilda pictured a small furry animal. At first, she didn't see anything on the ground where Jack was pointing. Then Gilda saw a round object that looked like an enormous, greenish-brown stone. Suddenly a head and legs emerged from the stone, and it began to move very slowly.

"It's a gopher tortoise," said Captain Jack. "She's a big one, too. I bet she's fifty years if she's a day."

The tortoise plodded forward, stopping to chew on some grass. *It's like a miniature dinosaur crossed with a tiny cow,* Gilda thought.

"Look at 'er grazing there. And see that big hole?" Captain Jack pointed to a sandy opening in the ground that was almost completely concealed by shrubs. "That's her burrow. It's probably about six feet deep down there. Sometimes snakes and other critters will move into those gopher burrows, too. That's why we call those tortoises 'landlords.'"

"Did you come here to look for tortoises?" Gilda thought the Mission seemed an odd place to do wildlife research.

"No—I just happened to be out on my boat fishing when I picked up my binoculars to look at what I thought might be a great white egret up in that tree right there. The bird flew away, but then I spied something big moving here on the ground, and I thought, 'I bet that's a gopher over there.' And lucky me—I was right. I like to keep my eye on these tortoises. They're endangered in Florida because their habitat has been all broken up by development."

"Would it make a good pet?" Gilda couldn't help thinking how attractive and unique this particular tortoise might look in Eugene's house. Plus, there wasn't any fur to cause allergies. *Maybe when it's not grazing outside, it could be trained to function as a living coffee table for glasses of sweet tea,* Gilda thought.

Captain Jack was obviously appalled. "Don't even think about it! It is totally illegal to catch one of these gophers and keep it as a pet."

"Oh, I wasn't *planning* on it. I just wondered."

"It's illegal to kill and eat it, too, in case you were wondering about *that*." Captain Jack glanced at Gilda's purse as if he wondered whether she might be concealing a tortoise-catching net or weapon of some kind.

"Do I look like the kind of person who goes around killing and eating endangered tortoises?"

"You'd be surprised at how many folks would eat one of these," said Captain Jack. He regarded Gilda with a hint of suspicion. "So what *are* you doing here?"

"I'm supposed to meet my mom and Mr. Pook for their wedding rehearsal this morning, but so far, I'm the only one here."

"Everyone else is late, huh?" Captain Jack chuckled. "Well, good for you for being on time." Captain Jack shaded his eyes and looked out over the water. "I'd better get back out there before the mullet stop biting."

"Mullet?"

"The fish." Jack waded back out to his boat. Gilda saw him rearrange some rather dangerous-looking knives and other fishing tools in his boat as he drifted away from shore. "You should come out to *my* ghost tour sometime!" he shouted across the water. "Bring the whole family!"

"I will!" said Gilda, making a mental note to suggest this idea to her mother. "Oh, and you should come to my mom's wedding! Evelyn and Debbie are invited, too!"

Captain Jack waved as he sailed farther away. Gilda suddenly wished that she had remembered to ask if he knew any stories about the ghost of the woman in white.

"So you're inviting pirates to the wedding?"

Gilda jumped; she hadn't heard Eugene approaching; suddenly, he was standing right behind her. "You startled me, Mr. Pook!"

"Nice dress," said Eugene, eyeing the dress Gilda had borrowed.

"Oh—thanks. I didn't mean to—" Gilda was about to explain that she hadn't originally intended to wear his vintage dress to the rehearsal, but Mr. Pook interrupted.

"So who was that man?" he asked.

"That was just Captain Jack. He leads one of the ghost tours on his boat."

"And he's coming to the wedding?"

"Um—I figured he might be fun to have at the reception since he knows so many interesting stories, but I don't even think he heard my invitation."

"I think it would be okay," said Mrs. Joyce, who had overheard the last part of the conversation. "We don't mind, do we, Pooky?"

That's way too embarrassing, Gilda thought to herself. *My stepfather must not be called "Pooky" in public!*

"Okay, but listen," said Eugene. "We're having a total of nine people at the wedding if you count the priest and two musicians. We are not planning a big reception."

"Actually, it's more like fourteen guests," said Gilda, counting on her fingers. "I might have neglected to tell you a teensy detail—that I invited a few other friends."

"What friends?"

"I thought we should invite your neighbors, Mary Louise and Darla."

"That's a good idea," Mrs. Joyce interjected. "We probably should invite them."

"Oh, and Evelyn Castle and her daughter, Debbie," Gilda added.

"And now this scruffy-looking pirate character, too?!" said Eugene. "Anyone else?"

"I'm pretty sure that's all."

"I'm confused, Eugene," said Mrs. Joyce. "Who were the nine guests before the people Gilda invited?"

Eugene counted on his fingers: "Well, there's you, me, Gilda, Stephen, the priest, two musicians, and the Furbos."

Mrs. Joyce looked perplexed. "Who are the Furbos?"

Gilda's ears perked up; something about "the Furbos" sounded familiar and important—possibly connected with a clue.

"Remember?" Eugene said. "They're the friends who

invited us over for a special dinner tonight—a real Minorcan feast."

Minorcans. Now Gilda remembered: Charlotte Furbo was Eugene's ex-girlfriend—*the one who left him at the altar!* "You're inviting the FURBOS to your wedding?!" Gilda blurted.

"Gilda, please," said Mrs. Joyce. "That was very rude."

"Does the name 'Charlotte Furbo' mean anything to you, Mom?"

Eugene's face turned red.

"No, it doesn't," said Mrs. Joyce.

"Charlotte Furbo happens to be the name of Eugene's old fiancée," said Gilda, doing her best not to meet Eugene's annoyed glare. "Mrs. Castle told me."

"Eugene," said Mrs. Joyce, "I'm not sure I feel comfortable having your ex-girlfriend at our wedding."

"I only invited Charlotte's *parents*," he said. "The Furbos are old friends—like family to me. I don't know if I told you this yet, Patty, but I didn't have a father at all when I was growing up." Eugene paused, looking across the bay as if his father might be out on the water somewhere. "One morning when I was a young child, my daddy got on the train at the St. Augustine station, and just never came back home. Well, it wasn't until I met Charlotte's daddy—Mr. Furbo—that I felt like I finally had a father. And you know—even though I'm a grown man, I value that. In fact, he taught me everything I know about fishing, cooking datil peppers—you name it. Just because Charlotte and I broke up doesn't mean I have to break up with my whole family now, does it?"

Listening to Eugene's story, Gilda had to admit she felt

sympathy for her mother's husband-to-be. *So Eugene lost his dad, too!* she thought. *In fact, Eugene's loss was much worse than mine. . . . His dad left on purpose!*

Gilda still didn't like Eugene much, but she decided she would try to cut him some slack since it probably wasn't his fault that he had no idea how to behave like a nice stepdad.

Mrs. Joyce's expression also softened with sympathy. "I can't imagine how hard that must have been, Eugene," she said. "And I suppose it was a very long time ago that you were engaged to Charlotte, wasn't it?"

"Yes, it was. Anyway, I'd like for you to meet the Furbos before the wedding. In fact, they suggested that we all come over for dinner tonight."

"Hello!"

Gilda, Mrs. Joyce, and Eugene turned to see the approach of an elderly priest who was followed by two musicians—a harpist and a guitar player. The harpist, who happened to be blind, wore dark sunglasses and walked arm-in-arm with the guitar player, who pushed the harp on little wheels while also carrying his guitar over his shoulder. The three had their hands full with music stands, folding chairs, and instruments.

"Good to see you after all these years, Eugene," said the priest, putting down two music stands and turning to Mr. Pook to shake his hand. "You've certainly changed!"

"It's been a long time, Father John."

"Yes, it has." The priest turned his attention to Mrs. Joyce. He squinted through his smile as he shook her hand, as if there were a puzzle in her face that he was trying to figure out. "You look *very* familiar," he said. "Are you from this area?"

"She's from Michigan," said Eugene hastily.

"I see."

"I'm Gilda," said Gilda, extending her hand. "I'm the daughter of the bride."

"And will you be participating in the ceremony?"

"I'm reading an original poem."

"Wonderful."

"It's called 'The Hour of Earthly Need.'"

"I see."

"My son will also be here for the ceremony," said Mrs. Joyce.

"He'll stop by if he can squeeze it into his schedule," Gilda whispered.

"Gilda, please," said Mrs. Joyce.

Gilda wondered if the priest had any interesting information about Eugene Pook's background. "Father John," Gilda asked, "do you and Mr. Pook know each other from church?"

"Actually, I performed Eugene's first wedding."

"His first wedding?!"

Both Eugene and Mrs. Joyce looked taken aback at this comment, and Father John quickly shook his head at his error. "What I meant to say was, I almost performed what *would* have been Eugene's wedding—or, what *should* have been. . . . Well, never mind that. Let's hope the second time does the trick. Right, Eugene?" Father John glanced at Mrs. Joyce nervously.

"Right."

"I'm sure that the two of you have both known each other long enough to be certain that this is the right move. No matter what the age of the participants, marriage is a serious, sacred, and brave decision."

Gilda coughed. *I bet he doesn't realize they only met face-to-face a couple weeks ago!* she thought.

"Good! Now—let's plan this ceremony so that everything goes perfectly *this time!*"

24

The Bones of the Holy

As she waited for her mother and Eugene to resolve their disagreement about whether the musicians should play "Jesu, Joy of Man's Desiring" or "Trumpet Voluntaire" to announce the beginning of the wedding ceremony, Gilda pulled out the crumpled piece of paper upon which she had written her wedding poem. To her surprise, her mother had said she loved the poem and Eugene had tolerated it (to her surprise, he commented that "the meter was off in a couple places"). Still it was about the best outcome she could hope for. She was considering whether to add another verse when a surprisingly cool breeze wafted up from the water and a large, white bird landed a short distance away, directly in front of a small chapel—the Shrine of Our Lady of La Leche.

What an amazing bird! Gilda thought, wishing that Captain Jack were there to see it. Curious, Gilda cautiously attempted to approach the bird, which stood very still and seemed to look directly at her. Something about the way it stared so intently at her made Gilda think of something she had read about how spirits can take the form of an animal to deliver a message. A moment later, the bird turned away and walked directly into the chapel through the open door.

How unusual! Gilda had a distinct and very Alice-in-Wonderland-ish feeling that the bird wanted her to follow.

The cool, silent shrine was devoted to motherhood, and at the altar, candles illuminated a painting of the Virgin Mary. Gilda looked around, but saw no sign of the large bird.

How could it just disappear? Gilda wondered. She still felt as if the bird—or *somebody*—wanted her to find something in the chapel. But what?

Gilda decided to light a prayer candle for her father.

"Dad," she whispered at the end of her prayer, *"if you can hear me, please help me figure out why I saw a ghost—and help me survive this wedding!"*

As she turned away from the prayer candles, Gilda spied something interesting on one of the wooden benches—a mysterious-looking book called *Relics of the Saints*. She picked up the heavy book and caught her breath when it immediately fell open to a page that had been marked with a small, white feather.

Is it a coincidence that I'm finding this feather right after seeing a white bird walk into the chapel? Or does this book contain a message that someone wants me to read?

Gilda scanned a passage near the feather:

The physical remains of saints, including bones and pieces of clothing, are considered relics worthy of preservation and veneration because of the miraculous protective powers and special magic of these physical remains. Note that the Catholic Church is not the only faith that follows such a tradition. Hindus and Buddhists also offer prayers to the Bones of the Holy. . . .

It's weird, Gilda thought, *how parts of people's bodies can become seemingly magical objects.* What would I have done if someone had given me the opportunity to keep one of Dad's bones with me forever—say a shinbone to carry in my backpack or a finger bone to wear on a necklace? Would it be gross? Or would it seem like an extra-special good-luck charm?

"Interesting book, isn't it?"

Startled, Gilda looked up to see a petite old woman dressed in a traditional nun's habit watching her. The woman's leathery, brown skin was etched in wrinkles, but her eyes were bright and youthful. "Oh—I was just looking," said Gilda, placing the book back on the bench.

"Please—you're welcome to read it."

Gilda read a couple more sentences, but she felt the old woman's searching eyes observing her.

"It's the energy of all the hundreds of prayers—the concentration of all those positive intentions—that gives those reliquary objects their power," said the nun.

"What do you mean?"

"We all know it's superstitious to believe in good-luck charms like four-leaf clovers, right? But miracles can happen. A four-leaf clover that has been the focus of many prayers could actually help protect you from evil and misfortune—especially if you believe that it can. It's just a way of physically carrying those prayers with you when you feel you're in danger."

Gilda thought of the pewter crucifix from Grandmother McDoogle. Maybe it was because her grandmother and great-grandmother had held it in their own hands for so many years that the object had the power to make her feel safer. It was similar to her typewriter: The knowledge that her father's fingers had spent many hours touching the keyboard seemed to give the old machine a special magic when Gilda used it to write letters or reports of her investigations.

"Here." The nun handed Gilda a candle inside a glass votive that bore a beautiful picture of an angel. "That's the archangel Michael—the slayer of demons. Take this for protection."

Gilda stared at the candle, feeling both intrigued and disturbed that the nun had spontaneously given it to her.

"We all know someone who needs some help and courage," said the nun.

Despite her interest in ghosts and psychic phenomena, stories about angels had always struck Gilda as saccharine fodder for women of an older generation, like her mother and Grandmother McDoogle. But now—standing in the old shrine with this elderly nun—the idea of calling on an angel for protection struck her as a potentially powerful idea.

She remembered a story her mother used to tell about guardian angels: "Everyone has one," her mother had said. "And sometimes when times are tough, I'll find a little white feather in an unexpected place, like in my purse or on the seat of my car. It sounds silly, but I know it's a message from my angel that everything is eventually going to be okay." *It's strange,* Gilda thought, *how Mom has always believed in angels but not ghosts, whereas I have always believed in ghosts but not necessarily angels.* She thought of Evelyn Castle's comment: "That's how the spirits in St. Augustine seem to me—more like ancestor spirits or guardian angels."

I guess believing that Dad can still somehow watch over me from heaven is kind of like believing in a guardian angel, Gilda thought. *Maybe that's what Darla needs, too—a guardian angel or some kind of psychic protection to make her feel safe from all the spirits she sees.*

"Thanks for your help," said Gilda. "I do know someone who needs this."

"I thought you might," said the nun. She handed Gilda some matches and a little bag for the candle. "Good luck to you," she said.

With the protection candle in hand, Gilda left the chapel with renewed determination. *If Darla and I work together, maybe she'll help me figure out who the woman in white is.*

25

The Woman Who Died Twice

It's got to be the white lilies, Patty. Trust me on this one."

"But, Eugene," Mrs. Joyce protested, "I like pink roses much better." The white lilies reminded Mrs. Joyce of the flowers that had topped her husband's casket at his funeral service. Their scent reminded her of the perfumed ladies who brought coffee cakes and casseroles to the house after the funeral.

"How about sunflowers?" Gilda suggested. "I love sunflowers." The argument between her mother and Eugene over flowers struck Gilda as particularly silly following the experience she'd just had at the chapel. She was still thinking about the woman in white, and wondering whether Eugene might know anything about her. *He says he doesn't believe in ghosts,* Gilda thought. *But I doubt it's possible to live here for so many years without having some unusual experiences in that house.*

"Eugene," Gilda ventured as they walked from the mission toward Water Street, "have you ever seen a ghost around here?"

"Like I told you before: There ain't no ghost but the Holy Ghost."

"Yes, I remember, but let me ask you this: Have you ever heard any *ghost stories* about a woman wearing a white dress who walks around your neighborhood?"

"Gilda, that's a bit macabre," said Mrs. Joyce.

"I know," said Gilda. "But someone told me she saw a ghost like that *near Mr. Pook's house*, so I just wondered."

Eugene frowned and regarded Gilda with a sidelong glance. "You do like your ghost stories, don't you, Miss Gilda?"

"Gilda has been interested in ghost hunting ever since her dad died," Mrs. Joyce explained, touching Gilda's arm gently.

"I can't say that I've ever heard any stories like that one...." Eugene stroked his mustache. "No, on second thought, I believe I have heard *one* story about the ghost of a woman dressed in white. The legend is that a young bride came down with yellow fever and fell into a coma. Her husband thought she was dead, so he quickly arranged for her funeral. The thing was, the husband wasn't too sad about his wife's death because he was secretly having an affair with another woman. Well, just when they were about to carry his wife to her grave to bury her, she just happens to surprise everyone by waking up in her coffin! It was considered a miracle. Everyone except the husband was happy; they all went home to celebrate, and that was that. Well, this husband decided that he couldn't wait around any longer for his wife to pass on a second time. He gradually began putting poison in her food, while telling everyone that she was sick with another terrible illness. And this time, when she died, he made sure that she stayed in the ground good and deep. She was buried in her wedding gown, which happened to be her favorite dress. And of course, the ghost story is that she comes back to haunt her husband wearing that dress."

"What an awful story!" said Mrs. Joyce.

"It's a fabulous story!" said Gilda. "I mean, it's horrifying, but it is an amazingly good ghost story."

"Glad you liked it," said Mr. Pook, clearly pleased that Gilda had enjoyed the story.

"Do you know the name of the family?" Gilda asked.

"What family?"

"I mean, the husband in the story—what was his name?"

"I have no idea. Of course, most of these stories are just local legends. Someone dies of natural causes and the next thing you know, people are seeing ghosts everywhere but the bathtub."

"Still," Gilda said, "it's a good story." *At least Mr. Pook knows a ghost story or two even if he doesn't believe in ghosts,* Gilda thought.

She pulled out her reporter's notebook and scribbled a note to herself:

> Could Eugene's ghost story explain the identity of the ghost I saw (the "woman in white")?
> Could this story explain the nightmare I had about the cemetery and someone being buried alive?

Gilda sighed as she closed her notebook. At the moment it seemed that every new clue was only making her feel more perplexed about the true nature of her mystery.

26

The Burial Ground

As Gilda, Eugene, and Mrs. Joyce approached Eugene's house, Gilda heard some unusual activity coming from Mary Louise's yard, so she peered over the fence to get a closer look. Mary Louise was engaged in a heated discussion with a young woman and a professorial-looking man with gray hair and glasses. The source of their concern was an enormous oak tree that had crashed to the ground during the nighttime storm, narrowly missing the roof of Mary Louise's house. The deep root system of the tree was exposed, and the tree's traumatic death had left a gaping pit in the yard.

"Wow!" Gilda declared. "Mom—Eugene—did you see what happened in Mary Louise's yard?"

"'Course we saw it," said Eugene. "She's lucky it didn't get her house; that's a big tree."

Gilda watched as the man squatted near the tree, carefully examining the soil around its roots.

How could I have missed seeing that fallen tree when I walked by their house this morning? Gilda wondered. *I guess I was so focused on trailing the woman in white that I didn't even notice anything else!*

Gilda realized with surprise that the young woman who appeared to be assisting the man was actually Debbie—the ghost-tour guide she had met the night before. Gilda hadn't recognized her at first with her dirt-smudged blue jeans, work boots, and her hair pulled back in a messy ponytail.

What is Debbie doing here? Gilda wondered, intrigued. "Hey, Mom," said Gilda, "I should introduce you to Debbie Castle. She's one of the people I invited to the wedding."

"Okay," said Eugene, "but Patty—we need to get ready for dinner in a few minutes. I still need to finish that new batch of datil-pepper jelly to take over to the Furbos."

Followed by her mother and Eugene, Gilda approached the group, curious to discover what they were discussing so earnestly.

"Once we complete a survey of the entire property, I reckon we'll need to do an excavation," said the man as he knelt near the root system of the tree and touched clumps of dirt gingerly. Broken pieces of painted pottery were spread on a blanket nearby.

"Hey, Mr. Pook—it looks like they found some artifacts under the tree!" Gilda expected Eugene to be delighted with this discovery, given his passion for antiques, but Eugene looked grim.

Gilda watched as Debbie picked up a clump of dirt and brushed it carefully, revealing a smooth, polished object that appeared to be some kind of tool. "Look," she exclaimed, "a pipe stem! I think it's made of some type of animal bone."

"Hello!" Mary Louise turned to greet Gilda, Eugene, and Mrs. Joyce. "As you can see, we had a rude awakening after our ghost tour last night. But these two archaeologists here are happy as clams."

"Thank you, Mary Louise!" said Debbie. "If you hadn't called me over here, I wouldn't have made my first big discovery!"

"Don't thank me; thank the tree for falling over," said Mary Louise. "At least it didn't land on my house."

"Hi, Debbie," said Gilda. "This is my mom—Patty Joyce. And I guess you already know Mr. Pook."

"I know your mother, Evelyn," said Eugene, shaking Debbie's hand.

"Congratulations to both of you on your engagement," said Debbie. "Oh, and this is Professor Bill Weller; he's a city archaeologist."

"So what do you think you've got here?" Eugene asked the archaeologist. "Anything worthwhile?"

"Based on the artifacts that have turned up just in the roots of this tree, we've got evidence of an old Indian village," said Professor Weller. "Chances are good there's a burial ground nearby, too. So far, we've found Timucuan artifacts. See that object Debbie's cleaning? It's a pipe stem made of animal bone. And this here is an old fishhook made of bone." Professor Weller held up the fishhook and then pointed out bits of dark-clay pottery, some of which was painted with a pattern that reminded Gilda of a checkerboard. "This looks like Timucuan pottery," he said. "We'll have to finish our survey first, but I reckon that the excavation site will extend into the adjacent property over there." He pointed to Eugene's house.

"That's my property you're thinking of digging up!" said Eugene. "I'm Eugene Pook."

"Looks like you may have the lucky distinction of living on top of an Indian burial ground," said Professor Weller.

"If that's the case," said Eugene, "I think it would be best to just leave it alone."

"Mr. Pook, we do our best to leave any human remains as undisturbed as possible," said Professor Weller.

"Seems to me that digging them up and dusting them off might disturb them a bit."

"A find like this could tell us a lot about prehistoric communities in St. Augustine. And of course, you never know what other valuables can turn up, too."

"Which I suppose you and your people would claim."

"The city would keep them only if you decided to donate them, sir. Which we encourage, of course."

"When are you expecting to dig up my yard? I'm having a wedding reception here in a couple days."

"You don't need to worry, Mr. Pook. We aren't going to dig anything until we survey the property, and we probably won't get to that for a week or so. We'll bring the documents for you to sign first."

"I still think it's wisest to leave the bones of the dead in peace."

"Mr. Pook," said the archaeologist, "we don't know if there are any dead over there yet, now, do we? We won't know that until we do an excavation."

"No," said Mr. Pook, gruffly, "I suppose we don't."

I wonder if Mr. Pook already knows there's a burial ground, but just isn't saying anything? Gilda thought. *It's hard to believe he's so concerned about disturbing the bones of the dead—unless he's really worried that he'll get in trouble for keeping that jawbone without notifying the city. . . . Or is he actually upset about awakening spirits who might not want their graves disturbed? Maybe Mr. Pook believes in ghosts more than he admits. . . .*

Just then, Gilda noticed a movement in an upstairs window of Mary Louise's house. It was Darla, peering down at the scene below. She quickly snapped the curtains shut when she saw Gilda staring up at her.

"Excuse me, Mary Louise," said Gilda. "Is it okay if I go ask Darla a question?"

"She's not feeling very well today, honey," said Mary Louise.

"I see," said Gilda, turning to march up to the front door. "In that case, I'd better go check on her."

Mary Louise watched as Gilda walked up the front steps and disappeared inside the house.

27

The Guardian Angel

Gilda found Darla in her very pink bedroom, sprawled on her bed and gazing down at her cell phone as she tapped out a text message. "Knock, knock," Gilda said, peering into Darla's room.

Darla practically jumped out of her skin at the mere sound of Gilda's voice. "Omigosh, you scared me half to death!" She grabbed a pillow and held it over her stomach as if protecting herself from an attack.

"Your mom told me I should come check on you," Gilda fibbed.

"I *told* Mama I don't feel well."

"What's wrong? Fingers sore from sending text messages?"

"No."

Gilda watched as Darla's fingers moved over the screen of her phone. "You're worried about this excavation, aren't you?"

Darla stopped tapping on her phone and sighed. "Maybe. I don't know."

"Did your mom tell you about the burial ground?"

She nodded. "She's all excited about it."

"Well, it is kind of interesting." Gilda walked slowly through

Darla's room, touching knickknacks here and there. "It's like uncovering an ancient mystery right here in your own front yard! Most kids would give their eyeteeth for that."

"What are eyeteeth?"

"I'm not sure; it's just an expression my grandmother used to say."

Darla continued staring at her cell phone, and Gilda was shocked to see tears slowly rolling down her cheeks. "What is it, Darla?" Gilda sat on the edge of Darla's bed.

"You don't understand. Seeing those bones moving around everywhere was not 'interesting'. It was horrible!"

Gilda looked around for a tissue, but couldn't find one. She opened her backpack and pulled out a napkin from the Spanish Bakery. "Here," she said, "blow."

Darla blew her nose loudly and sat up on the bed.

"Darla, I know you don't want me to talk to you about ghosts," said Gilda, "but I think I could help you." Gilda pulled *The Master Psychic's Handbook* out of her backpack.

Darla stared at the book as if it were a hairball lying on her bedspread.

"It's just a *book*, Darla; it won't *bite*. I learned just about everything I know about conducting psychic investigations from this book. Maybe if you learn to focus your skills more— and think more like an investigator, you won't be so scared."

"What do you mean?"

"Like, instead of just freaking out when you see a ghost, you can ask yourself: *'Why am I seeing this? What is this spirit trying to tell me?'* You'll also get better at just telling unwanted ghosts to leave you alone."

Darla picked up the worn book and flipped through the underlined, highlighted, and dog-eared chapters on topics including "Using a Pendulum," "Interpreting Your Dreams," "Conducting Séances," and "Automatic Writing." She had to admit feeling intrigued by some of the topics.

"You write in your books a lot, you know that?" Darla glanced warily at Gilda.

"I do that when I really like a book," said Gilda. "It drives my school librarian crazy, though, so now I just copy the sentences I like in a little notebook."

"Well," said Darla, "I guess I could take a look at it."

"Don't get too excited about it."

"I mean, I really appreciate it. Thanks."

"I got you something else, too." Gilda removed the archangel candle from her bag. "This is for special protection."

"A candle?"

"It's not just any candle; it's your special *guardian angel* candle. When you're feeling unsafe, you light this candle and say, 'Archangel Michael, please protect me and keep me safe from all danger and evil.'"

Darla took the candle and traced the image of the angel with her finger.

"You can say whatever words you want—just ask your guardian angel to protect you. Get it?"

"Does it work?"

Gilda wasn't at all sure it would work, but when she looked into Darla's hopeful, frightened eyes, she felt compelled to feign certainty. "Sometimes when I feel scared I think of my dad, who passed away, and I ask his spirit to help me get through it," she said. "And it's like having a guardian angel. So yes—it does work. It makes you brave."

"Why aren't you scared of ghosts—or anything?"

"I get scared all the time, Darla. But when that happens, I just try to talk myself out of it and continue my investigation. Sometimes I write myself a letter—kind of like a pep talk." *And sometimes I call Wendy in the middle of the night,* Gilda thought.

Darla stood up and placed the candle on her pink dresser. "Why do you want to help me with this stuff?"

The question caught Gilda off guard. *Why do I want to help her?* True, she wanted Darla's help with her investigation, but it was more than that. "I figured it must be scary to see all these spirits everywhere, but to have to pretend that you *aren't* seeing them. I mean, I don't know what I'd do if I didn't have my friend Wendy to talk to about some of the stuff that has happened during my investigations. . . . I guess I thought you could use a psychic 'big sister.'"

Darla just stared at her guardian angel candle and wore a lopsided grin that looked as if she were suppressing a very big smile. "Okay, I guess," she said. "I mean, it is hard not to be able to tell anyone when I see ghosts."

"Exactly. Plus, I figure that with *your* talent and *my* experience, we could be a great investigative team."

"What do you mean?"

"Darla, remember how you told me about the ghost in the white dress—the one you followed over to Mr. Pook's house when you saw all those bones?"

Darla nodded.

"Well, I saw her today. I'm sure it must be the same ghost."

"Did she show you the bones?" Darla whispered.

"No, she didn't," said Gilda. "But maybe if we did a séance together we could get some clues about her identity and figure out whether her spirit is trying to tell us something. Maybe she has a message about the Indian village—or something that happened later, like during the Civil War. If we uncover her story, seeing her won't feel so scary."

Darla nodded. "But Gilda—I really don't want to do stuff with television cameras and ghost-hunting shows."

"Definitely not. I hate those shows." Gilda secretly felt that she wouldn't mind being featured on one of the ghost-hunting shows, but nobody had ever invited her.

"And don't say anything to Mama about this stuff either."

"Got it. Mum's the word."

"What does that mean?"

"I won't say anything."

"Good."

"So listen. Read *The Master Psychic's Handbook*, and then we'll get together to try a séance, okay?"

"I guess." Darla suddenly looked doubtful.

"Darla, if you don't face up to these spirits who keep trying to get your attention, you'll have to go through your life always feeling scared—always trying to hide from things you don't want to see."

"Okay," said Darla. "We can try it."

"Great. Now I have to get ready to have dinner at my mother's fiancé's ex-girlfriend's parents' house."

Darla wrinkled her nose. "Sounds complicated."

"That's an understatement, Darla. Well, toodles. Happy reading!"

After Gilda left, Darla glanced around the room before picking up the book of matches Gilda had left. She struck a match and carefully lit her guardian angel candle with a shaking hand.

28

Aren't You Jealous?

Dear Wendy:

I laid out in the sun all day and I am super burned! I'm hoping it will turn into a tan by the time I get back to school, though.

Well, my hand hurts from typing, so I've gotta go. Time to read another fashion mag, flip myself over, and fry the other side!

JUST KIDDING!!!

I remain your freckled, shade-loving friend.

NEWS FLASH:

Remember the Woman in White story I was telling you about--that ghost-woman wearing a bridal gown that the neighbor-girl Darla saw? Well, this morning I saw her. That's right: I, Gilda Joyce, SAW A GHOST. As you know, this is a big deal for me, because I don't usually see ghosts except in my dreams. Sure, I get messages in other ways, but this was highly unusual. I still don't know who this ghostly woman in white is, but I have a couple ideas:

1. She may be the ghost of a woman who was murdered by her husband and then buried in her wedding gown.

2. She might have been a yellow fever victim who died on her wedding day (incidentally, I had a weird dream about someone being buried alive in the "yellow fever" cemetery in St. Augustine. I also know that a lot of the Timucua Indians who lived here died of yellow fever.).

3. She might be an alien from outer space who is plotting to steal all the chocolate, peanut butter, and banana sandwiches on earth. (Just testing you there to make sure you're awake.)

OTHER NEWS:

I now have a psychic "little sister." (Don't worry; she's totally potty trained.) So far, it's kind of like a two-person sorority where I help her develop her psychic skills and she helps me talk to ghosts. (At least I'm hoping she will.) I've always thought that I'd be a better big sister than I am a little sister because I'm so good at teaching people stuff, you know? (I can hear your snort-

laugh all the way from Michigan, Wendy, so
have some tact.) But seriously, I think I
might be able to help Darla become a real
psychic.

Are you jealous??

Are you SURE you're not jealous?

Not even a teensy little bit?

Crikey! I can't believe I almost forgot
to mention the other piece of ho-hum news!
Why does NOTHING EXCITING ever happen to
me?! (That was sarcasm, incidentally.)

Today archaeologists began excavating
the property next to Mr. Pook's house
because they found evidence of an Indian
village there. They think there might be
an Indian burial ground nearby as well--
possibly on Mr. Pook's property.

Yes, Wendy, the horror-movie
implications of staying in a house that's
probably built on an Indian burial ground
are not lost on me. (Have I mentioned that
this house may have also been used as a
hospital during the Civil War?) If you
don't hear from me in a few days, send some
backup down here to see if we're all still
alive.

Seriously.

I have been wondering whether some of
the odd happenings around Mr. Pook's house

have any connection with the Indian jawbone
he keeps on display in the glass-topped
coffee table in his living room. (Can you
believe it?! I mean, really. Come to think
of it, I've been meaning to ask my mom what
she thinks of that little coffee-table
display.) Well, Mr. Pook is going to be
pretty surprised when a bunch of his stuff
gets thrown out and replaced with Hummel
figurines after the wedding! You know how
when my mom gets in a bad mood, she starts
throwing out everything in sight and you
really have to keep an eye on stuff like
your manuscript pages and extra boxes of
Twinkies? All I can say is: good luck
keeping a human jawbone around during one
of Patty's famous cleaning binges, Mr.
Pook!

Well, I'd better be going, Wendy. I'm
off to dinner at the home of some true
Minorcans! (Hold your questions, please;
I'll explain later.)

Your friend and colleague,
Gilda Joyce

29

Gopher Stew

When Gilda, her mother, and Eugene arrived at the Furbos' large house on the outskirts of St. Augustine, Mr. Furbo greeted Eugene with a slap on the back. "So, after all these years, Eugene finally finds a girl to marry him!"

Mr. Furbo's stocky physique, blunt features, and ruddy skin reminded Gilda of a rough sculpture molded from clay. She noticed prominent scars on his hands and arms; she guessed they were the result of farming accidents. During the drive to the Furbos' house, Eugene had explained how the Furbo family owned several hundred acres of land on the outskirts of St. Augustine. "They know this land like the back of their hands, and they've been through everything here—good times and bad," Eugene had said. "They're tough folks—some of the most hardworking people I know."

Mr. Furbo turned to Mrs. Joyce, gripped her shoulders, and held her at arm's length, scrutinizing her appearance: "Well I'll be . . ." He seemed to blanch for a moment, as if he found Mrs. Joyce's appearance upsetting in some way.

"What's the matter, Bob?" Eugene asked.

"You do have a *type* when it comes to the ladies, don't you, Eugene?"

Gilda's ears perked up at this comment.

"'Course, she looks *older* than Charlotte," he added.

"Thanks a lot!" said Mrs. Joyce, laughing nervously.

"Oh, he means it as a compliment, Patty," was Eugene's hasty clarification.

"Come here, Theresa," Mr. Furbo called. "See if Eugene's new fiancée doesn't look like she could be Charlotte's older sister! Or aunt!" It was difficult to tell whether Mr. Furbo was delighted or annoyed with Mrs. Joyce's resemblance to his daughter. On one hand, he seemed happy to meet Mrs. Joyce—almost as if his own daughter had stepped into his house for a visit. On the other hand, there was an angry edge to his voice that suggested a reprimand—as if Mrs. Joyce's appearance in his home was an unpleasant reminder of something he wanted to forget.

Is he angry that Eugene picked a woman who resembles his daughter? Gilda wondered. *But why, exactly?*

Dressed in pearls, a white blouse, blue jeans, and an apron, Mrs. Furbo emerged from the kitchen. She was a petite woman with an olive complexion and quick, birdlike movements. She gave Mrs. Joyce a fierce, hard stare and then disappeared back into the kitchen without smiling or even saying hello to her guests.

"Hello there, Theresa!" Eugene called after Mrs. Furbo.

What kind of Southern hospitality was that?! Gilda thought. Clearly, the Furbos had very mixed feelings about this visit from Eugene and his new family-to-be.

"Something smells wonderful in that kitchen!" Eugene added.

"We'll see when we taste it!" Mrs. Furbo snapped from inside the kitchen.

"Well, Bob, as you already know, this here is my fiancée, Patty—the one I've been telling you about," said Eugene. "And this is her daughter, Gilda."

"Nice to meet you," said Gilda. "We've been enjoying your datil-pepper recipes." Gilda figured Mr. Furbo might warm up to her if she shared one of his interests.

"Well, good!" he said, clearly delighted at the mention of datil peppers. "I do love the pepper jelly!"

Mr. Furbo led the group to the dining table where he poured drinks from a pitcher for everyone. "So, Eugene. You waited to get married till you finally found another one like Charlotte!"

Again, Gilda detected a note of anger in Mr. Furbo's voice—or was it fear? She couldn't quite explain it, but there was something unusual about his tone.

Eugene shifted uncomfortably. "Well, that's not exactly—"

"No, I can understand it." Mr. Furbo looked at Eugene very directly. "Charlotte was a very special girl. Despite what she did."

"What, exactly, did Charlotte do?" Gilda asked. *It's weird how he talks about his daughter as if she doesn't exist anymore,* she thought.

"Gilda, that might be a personal question," Mrs. Joyce warned.

"Oh, most everybody in town knows that Charlotte left

Eugene the night before his wedding," Mr. Furbo said. "Actually, she left *all* of us that night."

"It was a long time ago," said Eugene, staring mournfully into his drink.

"What do you mean, 'She left all of us'?" Gilda asked. She sensed her mother's displeased look (*Don't ask prying questions!*), but she simply *had* to find out more. *Something about this situation is fishy,* she thought.

"Charlotte moved away to Europe without much of a warning," said Eugene, without elaborating further.

"How often do you and Mrs. Furbo see your daughter since she moved?" Mrs. Joyce asked, doing her best to steer the conversation toward a friendly, polite tone.

"Not often," said Mr. Furbo.

"We never see her!" Mrs. Furbo snapped from the kitchen.

Gilda met her mother's eyes across the table. For once, she and her mother were in complete agreement. *There is something very weird about that,* Gilda thought.

"In fact," said Mr. Furbo, "we're coming up on the twenty-year anniversary of the last time we saw Charlotte."

Gilda felt baffled. It was hard to imagine having two living parents and not seeing them for two whole decades. *Did Charlotte and her parents have a fear of flying? Were the plane tickets too expensive?* Clearly, there was some crucial piece of information that everyone refused to talk about. *JUST TELL ME ALREADY!* Gilda wanted to scream. *WHAT DID CHARLOTTE DO?!*

"So, Mr. Furbo . . ." Gilda said, doing her best to sound ladylike and tactful, "have you ever thought of *visiting* Charlotte?"

"No," he said. "Can't say that I have." The air in the room felt prickly with tension.

"She made her choice," Mrs. Furbo snapped, still speaking from the kitchen.

"Um—so it sounds like you didn't want her to move to Europe?" Gilda guessed.

"Among other things," said Mr. Furbo.

Are they still mad that she didn't marry Eugene? Gilda wondered.

Mr. Furbo squinted at Mrs. Joyce and again shook his head with disbelief. "If Charlotte was in this room right now, I'd swear that she and you were sisters."

"Do you have any pictures of Charlotte?" *Maybe looking at some old photos will get them talking about what actually happened in the past,* Gilda thought.

Mrs. Joyce frowned at Gilda, clearly desperate to abandon the topic of Charlotte Furbo. But Gilda couldn't resist; she simply had to see what Charlotte looked like after all of this cryptic discussion about her.

Mr. Furbo turned to an antique side table, opened a drawer, and pulled out a leather photograph album. "I believe the last picture we have of Charlotte was her engagement photo," he said, flipping through the pages. "But I don't look at these anymore."

Mr. Furbo thrust the photo album across the table toward Gilda. "There she is," he said.

Gilda looked at the black-and-white photograph of a pretty young woman with dark, wavy hair that tumbled over her shoulders. *He's right,* she thought. *She does resemble Mom, even though Mom looks much older.* Something about the girl's hazel eyes and tentative smile looked very much like the pictures Gilda had seen from her mother's youth. On the other hand, Gilda thought that Charlotte's look was dreamier—more romantic and feminine than the old photos of Patty Joyce that usually featured bad hairstyles, blue jeans, and cheap platform shoes.

"She's cute," said Mrs. Joyce, a hint of jealousy in her voice.

"Stop complimenting yourself," Mr. Furbo joked.

Mrs. Furbo emerged from the kitchen with bowls of chowder balanced on a silver tray. "I made your favorite, Eugene!" Mrs. Furbo announced.

Maybe she's in a better mood now that she's done cooking, Gilda thought.

"Patty and Gilda, you're in for a treat," said Eugene. "Traditional Minorcan clam chowder!"

"It's not as traditional as we'd *like* it to be," said Mrs. Furbo.

"Right. The old favorite was actually the gopher stew," Eugene explained.

"Gophers?!" Mrs. Joyce froze, peering down at her bowl of soup as if it might contain snakes.

"Mom, he means the gopher *tortoise*," said Gilda, proud that she had already learned this bit of local history from Captain Jack.

"Oh," said Mrs. Joyce, who clearly didn't feel much better about the idea of gopher tortoises. "Well. I don't believe we have gopher tortoises in Michigan."

"You didn't tell me they were from *Michigan*!" Mr. Furbo put down his spoon and fixed Eugene with an accusing stare.

"What's wrong with Michigan?" Gilda asked.

"What's *not* wrong with Michigan?"

Gilda sensed that he was only teasing, but she restrained an impulse to get into an argument in defense of her home state. *I need to stay on his good side if I'm going to learn any top secret information about Charlotte,* she reminded herself.

"We always had the gopher tortoise stew at holidays and family reunions," Mrs. Furbo lamented. "Then they went and made it illegal to eat it."

So these are the people who might eat a gopher tortoise if they got a chance, Gilda thought. She remembered how Captain Jack had looked at her suspiciously. *"You'd be surprised at how many folks would eat one of these,"* he had said.

"The gopher tortoise is an endangered species," Eugene explained. "Or close to endangered, anyway."

"Oh, there's plenty of 'em!" Mrs. Furbo flicked her hand with a dismissive wave. "I've seen 'em, anyway. You just have to know where to look."

Gilda wondered what Captain Jack would say if he were here at the table. She guessed he would explain how the gopher tortoise habitat had been broken up by parking lots and highways. She also sensed that there would be no end to the argument if she attempted to stick up for the rights of gopher tortoises—or for that matter, anything else that threatened to change some of the old family traditions.

"Go on—dig in!" said Mr. Furbo.

Eugene slurped some clam chowder, leaving a milky stain on his mustache. "This is mighty good, Theresa!"

Mrs. Furbo shook her head. "It's not near as good as the gopher stew would have been."

"Now, let me tell you something about gopher tortoises," said Mr. Furbo, addressing Gilda as if he were about to begin an educational lecture. "Back when my daughter, Charlotte, was little, whenever I found a gopher burrow on our property, I'd dig a hole about four feet down to wherever it was hiding in the burrow. Then I'd grab little Charlotte by the legs, pick her up, and lower her headfirst down into the gopher burrow. From a young age, she was a natural. In a minute she'd grab that big ole tortoise and pull it out for me. Then we'd go prepare the gopher stew together. . . ." His voice trailed off, and he looked suddenly stricken with the weight of a terrible memory.

Is he nostalgic for the old days when Charlotte was around? Or is he just sad about not being able to eat gopher tortoises? Gilda wondered. To the Furbos, the animal seemed to represent a lost history— perhaps a simpler life that had disappeared.

"It sounds like you miss seeing your daughter," said Mrs. Joyce, gently.

Mr. Furbo shook his head, as if trying to physically shake off the sad feelings. "No," he said with surprising emphasis. "*She* made her choice."

Mrs. Furbo looked grim.

"What *choice*?" Gilda asked, now feeling as if she was going to die of curiosity if someone didn't tell her the whole story about Charlotte soon. *Whatever the choice was,* she thought, *it seemed to have had the effect of ending her relationship with her entire family.*

"Bob," said Eugene, obviously hoping to change the topic of conversation, "why don't you tell Patty and Gilda how you used to make the gopher stew?"

"But——" Gilda was still desperate to talk about Charlotte. She was sure that Mr. Furbo had been on the verge of revealing some juicy piece of information.

"Well, after you manage to catch the gopher," said Mr. Furbo, "you whack it real hard on the back of the shell so the legs come out. Then you grab a hatchet and cut down each side, take off the toenails, cut out the guts, and don't forget to eat the eggs—that's the best part. Then just cook it up with some datil pepper, onions, bacon fat, garlic, potatoes, and whatever else you want to throw in there. Charlotte just loved it when she was a kid."

"Until she became one of those animal rights people and wouldn't help you do that no more," said Mrs. Furbo angrily. She regarded Gilda and Mrs. Joyce with a deadpan expression. "*You* aren't vegetarians, are you?"

"If it walks, I eat it," Gilda quipped, half wondering if they might have some poor gopher tortoise hiding in the kitchen that she would be forced to kill to prove herself.

"Because we don't allow vegetarians in our house."

I think she might actually be serious, Gilda thought. "Is Charlotte still a vegetarian?" Gilda had struck a nerve; there was a silence before anyone answered.

"We don't know," said Mrs. Furbo. She stood up abruptly and began to gather empty soup bowls. She paused and stared at Mrs. Joyce's virtually untouched soup. "What's the matter? You're not hungry?"

"Don't worry; there's no gopher tortoises in there," Mr. Furbo joked.

"It's delicious," said Mrs. Joyce, who was suddenly fighting a queasy stomach that had more to do with nerves than the clam chowder.

"Small appetite, huh?" Mr. Furbo chuckled. "Sounds like Patty here is like Charlotte in more ways than just looks!"

"I'll leave that chowder there for you to *finish*," said Mrs. Furbo, still frowning at Mrs. Joyce as if she were a petulant child. "It's perfectly good chowder, and I don't want it to go to waste!"

"Thank you, Theresa, but I'm not your child," Mrs. Joyce blurted, shocking everyone at the table.

Even Gilda was surprised. Her mother normally reserved her most direct, critical statements for her children. *Uh-oh,* Gilda thought. *Sounds like the wedding stress is starting to get to Mom.*

"Oh ho! You'd better watch this one, Eugene," Mr. Furbo joked, pointing an accusing finger at Mrs. Joyce. "Next thing you know, she'll up and leave you for a colored man just like Charlotte did!"

The atmosphere in the room turned brittle. Gilda's jaw dropped with surprise at the revelation of this detail about Charlotte's past, not to mention the reality of lingering racist views in the Furbo family. Mrs. Joyce lowered her eyes as if she were a teenager who had just been reprimanded by an authoritarian father. Eugene seemed to concentrate very hard on the process of buttering his dinner roll.

Gilda was torn between an intense desire to escape the room and never return and a wish that her mother would say something—anything—to let both Mr. Furbo and Eugene know what she thought of the tactless comment.

Taking a deep breath, Gilda resolved to turn her attention back to the task of finding out more about Charlotte. She had to make sure she had this story straight. "Mr. Furbo," she said, cautiously, "are you saying that Charlotte left Eugene to move to Europe with an African-American man?"

Mr. Furbo regarded Gilda with suspicion. "You can call it whatever you want, but the fact is that Charlotte ran off with a Black man, and I personally couldn't stand for that."

So it wasn't just a bad breakup that happened between Eugene and Charlotte, Gilda thought. *Charlotte had a total falling-out with her entire family!* Gilda looked at Mrs. Furbo to gauge whether she shared her husband's views, but her face was inscrutable.

"I couldn't forgive Charlotte for what she did," said Mr. Furbo. "She knew how I felt about *that*. I told her; 'You come home when you're done with this nonsense.'" He shook his head and tossed a napkin on the table with a violent gesture of disgust. "Well. She never did come home. She made her choice."

Gilda felt a wave of sadness and something close to nausea. *It must have been hard for Charlotte to have Mr. and Mrs. Furbo as her parents when she was a kid,* Gilda thought. *I mean, what if my parents had said that Wendy's family should "move back to China" or that I shouldn't spend so much time with her?* Gilda tried to imagine what it would feel like to have parents who would make her choose between her relationship with a boyfriend— or any friend—and her family. *My family would never do that,* she realized. They might be mad at me, but they'd never tell me, "Don't come home."

Maybe I'm lucky, Gilda thought. *I mean, my family definitely isn't perfect—Stephen is a little selfish and Mom doesn't always believe my stories and Dad is dead and gone—but at least we're all free to be ourselves.*

One thing was certain: The situation with Charlotte was far more complicated than Gilda had imagined. She hadn't expected the ghosts of a racially segregated past to play a role in this family drama.

"She made her choice," Mrs. Furbo repeated. "She wanted nothing to do with us anymore."

But you forced her to choose, Gilda thought. *And now she's gone.*

Gilda now understood the hidden sadness that pervaded the Furbos' environment: Even as Mrs. Furbo served traditional favorites like shrimp with datil-pepper sauce and Mr. Furbo and Eugene spoke of favorite hunting trips, beautifully carved antique rifles, and the heroic survival stories of the Minorcan community in Florida, Gilda sensed that the reminiscences were not enough to overcome a missing piece. *They won't admit it,* Gilda thought, *but they miss Charlotte.*

Without warning, the room went dark and something crashed to the floor. "Oh!" Mrs. Joyce cried out in surprise.

"What the blazes—" Mr. Furbo muttered.

"Must be a blown fuse," Mrs. Furbo suggested.

"It's the wiring in these old houses," Eugene suggested. "I have the same problem at my place lately."

"Well, let's not just sit here like bumps on a log," said Theresa. "I'll get a flashlight."

Then, just as suddenly, all the lights came back on.

"That was strange," said Mr. Furbo, gazing up at the overhead light fixture.

"Oh, I'm sorry!" Mrs. Joyce had just realized that her bowl

of clam chowder had crashed to the floor after the lights went out, shattering and splattering soup everywhere. "That bowl just seemed to jump off the table!"

"I'll get some paper towels." Theresa sounded annoyed; she clearly didn't believe that Mrs. Joyce's bowl had "jumped off the table."

"Looks like you might have a poltergeist here, Mr. Furbo," Gilda ventured, partly to gauge his reaction. "Does this sort of thing happen often?"

"There ain't no ghost but the Holy Ghost," was Mr. Furbo's terse reply.

So that's where Eugene learned that phrase, Gilda thought. But before she could ask any more questions, they were interrupted by the horribly loud metallic clatter of a large pot toppling from the kitchen stove onto the floor.

"Good night! Are you okay in there, Theresa?" Mr. Furbo called.

A moment later, a grim-looking Mrs. Furbo emerged from the kitchen, her apron completely soaked with clam chowder.

"Don't you say anything," she snapped at Mr. Furbo.

"You're supposed to put it in your mouth, not take a bath in it!"

Gilda suppressed a sudden urge to giggle; Mrs. Furbo clearly didn't see any humor in the situation.

With everyone's help, Mrs. Furbo focused on cleaning up the spilled soup, refusing to speculate about the possible causes of the strange series of events. "I don't buy into that ghost-tour trash that goes on in the city these days," was her snappish reply to Gilda's query about a possible ghost in the house.

Nevertheless, Gilda noticed that something about Mrs. Furbo's demeanor had changed following the poltergeist activity: Her hands now shook slightly as she cleared away dishes and served a peach pie for dessert. At the end of the meal, she joined her guests for pie and coffee, but her eyes darted strangely, as if scanning the room for the presence of some predator who might be lurking in the shadows.

30

The Freedom Trail

To: MRS. RABIDO
From: GILDA JOYCE
RE: TRAVELOGUE ASSIGNMENT ENTRY #3

Dear Mrs. Rabido:

I hope you're doing well and managing to keep your spirits up during my absence.

What have I been doing, you ask? Where, pray tell, is my latest travelogue submission?

Sorry to keep you waiting, Mrs. Rabido, but I happen to be embroiled in a very perplexing mystery that seems to involve several ghosts, not to mention some very unnerving wedding plans. I mean, it's not as bad as an in-class essay, but it's no picnic either, just in case you're picturing me sipping piña coladas down here on the beach. In fact, I have not been to the beach a single time since my arrival (which I don't really mind because I burn really easily). However, you'll be happy to know that this evening I did have the opportunity to dine with an older gentleman named Bob Furbo who is a descendant of the colonial St. Augustine settlers, loosely grouped as "the Minorcans."

Tonight I learned that the lives of this community have been closely tied to the natural Florida landscape. For example, during the Depression years when hardly anybody had money to spend, Bob Furbo's family found plenty of fish, gopher tortoises, and sea turtle eggs to eat for free—right in their own backyard. "In fact," Mr. Furbo noted, "when I was a kid, we'd sometimes catch a gopher tortoise and take it down to the grocery store to trade it for some bread and meat. And sometimes the guy behind the counter would give us back a smaller tortoise as change because he didn't have any money either."

Well, Mrs. Rabido, after a life of struggles many old-timers like Mr. Furbo feel that they've paid their dues and don't want anyone telling them what to do or what to eat. For example, if you happen to catch one of them sneaking a handful of sea turtle eggs from the beach to eat raw, you'll know it's not so much a sign of disrespect for the law as it is a declaration of love for the slimy reptilian flavors of their hometown. Nevertheless, the law is the law, Mrs. Rabido, so don't let me catch you or any of your friends sneaking some turtle eggs into the teachers' lounge if you get a job down here!

THE FREEDOM TRAIL IN ST. AUGUSTINE:

Mrs. Rabido, my report would not be complete without some mention of the important Civil Rights struggles that have taken place here in St. Augustine. (In this section of my paper, I'll refrain from quoting Mr. Furbo. Let's just say that a handful of the old-timers have a way of reminding us both how far we've come and how far we have to go when it comes to viewing each other as equals.)

As I write this entry, we're driving past the atmospheric "Old Market" in the city, where people of all nationalities and colors are just sitting outside, playing chess, talking, or walking hand in hand to the restaurants. It's weird to think that there was actually a time when this same place was called "The Old Slave Market"—a place where people could actually be bought and sold like objects in a store.

It's also hard to imagine that back in the year 1964, Martin Luther King was arrested just for trying to enter a "whites only" restaurant right here in St. Augustine.

I think it's hard to imagine how scary and downright unpleasant it must have felt to walk into a restaurant and be asked to leave just because of a simple fact of your appearance. The only personal experience I can compare it to is one time when my family was asked to leave a fancy restaurant in Grosse Pointe because my dad wasn't wearing a dinner jacket. (We didn't realize the restaurant had a dress code.) Mind you, Mrs. Rabido, I'm not saying that this was anything even close to being the victim of racist laws in the Jim Crow South! I'm just saying that I remember the feeling of shame and anger we all had as we filed out of that place with all the other customers just staring at us. It made me want to throw eggs at the building (which Dad also wanted to do, but Mom wouldn't let us).

Mrs. Rabido, I guess we're lucky to live in a time when people are free to pursue their dreams and go anywhere they want in this country. But some of us are not completely free, Mrs. Rabido. I'm beginning to see how the ghosts of a painful past still drag their chains through a few of these old houses.

On that somber note, I am signing off and retreating to my boudoir, Mrs. Rabido!

Sleep tight; don't let the bedbugs bite!

GILDA JOYCE

31

The Message in the Dream

The rope tightened around Gilda's ankles as she descended headfirst into the open pit, flashlight in hand.

"Do you see it?"

"Not yet," she said, feeling unsure what she was looking for.

"Grab it when you see it," the voice said. "Grab it, and pull it out!"

Down she went, farther and farther underground. I can see it now, she thought; I can see the layers of history. Lizards and spiders scuttled around her, then came the generations of skeletons.

Some of the skeletons lay prone, holding crosses; others sat upright, as if buried sitting around a campfire. Then she glimpsed something smooth and gleaming—the shell of the endangered gopher tortoise. *How strange to find one burrowing so deep below the surface—even below the secret graves,* she thought.

"Grab it!" a faint voice shouted from above. "Grab it and kill it!"

"I can't," she said. She didn't want to kill it.

"Give 'er here—we'll take care of it. Don't let 'er get away!" The voice now came from below. Gilda found herself looking down into the Furbos' kitchen, where she saw Mr. and Mrs. Furbo holding rifles. They stood on either side of the kitchen table, where they had placed the tortoise. "Give it a good whack on the back," said Mr. Furbo. Gilda squeezed her eyes shut, not wanting to see.

"Help!" It was a woman's voice—a voice that sounded familiar.

"Finish the job," said Mrs. Furbo.

Gilda opened her eyes just in time to see the Furbos backing away from the table. To her surprise, there was no tortoise. Instead, a young woman lay unconscious on the table, her long, white dress stained in blood. Gilda recognized her face: It matched the picture Mr. Furbo had shown her—the photograph of his daughter, Charlotte.

It's Charlotte, Gilda thought. *And she's dead!*

Gilda awoke with a start and immediately sat up in bed. *I have to write down everything I saw in the dream before I forget!* she thought. Gilda often picked up clues to her mysteries through images in her dreams, and she felt certain that this had been a psychic dream.

TO: GILDA JOYCE
FROM: GILDA JOYCE
RE: PSYCHIC DREAM REPORT

ALERT!!
NEW HYPOTHESIS FOLLOWING PSYCHIC DREAM!!
IS IT POSSIBLE THAT CHARLOTTE FURBO IS DEAD??

IS IT POSSIBLE THAT THE FURBOS KILLED THEIR OWN DAUGHTER?!

The dream:

In my dream, I saw Mr. and Mrs. Furbo holding guns. They stared down at their daughter, Charlotte, who was lying on a table, apparently dead. She wore a bloodstained white dress.

When I awoke, I had two questions in my mind: 1) What if Charlotte never made it to Europe with her new boyfriend after all? 2) What if she was murdered?

The idea that the Furbos killed their own daughter is almost too awful to consider, but it's also true that the Furbos had a motive to kill Charlotte (albeit a disturbing one): They were furious with her for breaking off her engagement to Eugene right before the wedding. Maybe their racist feelings made the situation all the more volatile. On top of everything, they clearly have easy access to guns.

Of course, having a motive and owning a rifle doesn't necessarily mean they committed a crime, just as a psychic dream doesn't constitute hard evidence or proof. Still, it's a hypothesis that bears further investigation.

NEXT STEPS:
1. Find some hard evidence about Charlotte Furbo's whereabouts. Research needed.
2. Question the Furbos in more detail.

3. Ask Darla if she'll help me do a séance. I'm curious whether she would uncover anything about the Furbos in connection with the woman in white and Charlotte.

IS IT POSSIBLE THAT THE WOMAN IN WHITE IS THE GHOST OF CHARLOTTE FURBO?

32

Halloween Day

Gilda had read somewhere that people in the old days wore masks and costumes on Halloween in order to trick evil spirits into leaving them alone. Given the hidden graveyards and other dark secrets around the neighborhood, Gilda figured she might need some protection before attempting a séance in St. Augustine, so she put on her Southern belle costume.

Once dressed in her corseted Civil War–era petticoats and wig with ringlets, Gilda felt safer for some reason, and newly determined to find out more about Charlotte Furbo and the woman in white.

Maybe Wendy can research the whereabouts of Charlotte Furbo on her computer. I need to verify whether she's actually alive or not. If she is alive, I definitely want to ask her some questions!

Of course, the research wouldn't be easy, since Gilda didn't even know what European city Charlotte was supposed to be in.

"I can't talk right now," Wendy whispered. "I'm in the school library."

"Already? It's not even seven thirty A.M."

"Some of us attend school during the day."

"But why are you in the library so early?"

"A little thing called a research paper. I'm doing my index cards."

"Gotta love the index cards." Gilda thought guiltily of the untouched index cards she had brought with her in her backpack. When she got home she would have to spend long hours in the library catching up on her research project. So far, she hadn't even settled on a topic.

"So how's the beach?"

"What beach?"

"Aren't you in Florida?"

"I've been working, Wendy. And I actually need your help with something. If you have a second to get on the computer, I need you to find anything you can about someone named Charlotte Furbo."

Gilda explained the story of how Charlotte left Eugene for another man and then supposedly moved to Europe. "But I now have a theory that Charlotte might have been murdered instead," she said.

Gilda told Wendy about the ghostly woman in white whom she and Darla had seen, and the dream about Mr. and Mrs. Furbo standing next to their daughter's dead body.

"I promise I'll check it out as soon as I have a chance, but I gotta go now," Wendy whispered. "Ms. Zucconi is looking at me, and she's going to take away my phone any second now; I'll send you a message later, okay?"

"Wait—Wendy?"

"What?"

"Happy Halloween. I'm wearing the Southern-belle costume, just so you know."

"Happy Halloween, Gilda. I'm not wearing any costume, and I'm hanging up now."

Mrs. Joyce stood in the middle of the kitchen, staring into space. She had walked into the room several minutes before, but couldn't remember what she had been doing.

"Patty-Cakes?"

Startled, Mrs. Joyce came to her senses. She turned to see Eugene standing in the kitchen doorway, staring at her with a worried expression.

"I've been sitting out there in the car waiting for you," said Eugene. "Are you okay?"

"You were waiting for me?"

"Remember? We have to pick up Stephen at the airport! And then we have our final wedding preparations."

"Oh—I guess I forgot what I was doing." Mrs. Joyce walked unsteadily to the sink and poured herself a glass of cold water. She couldn't for the life of her remember what she had been doing in the kitchen—why she had come into the room in the first place.

"You look beautiful in that dress," said Eugene, admiring the vintage outfit he had selected from his collection for her to wear.

"Thank you." Mrs. Joyce liked the dress, but it also made her feel strange, as if she were wearing someone else's clothes. *I don't feel at all like myself today,* she thought. Normally she would have dismissed the feeling as a result of sleep deprivation or stress, but she was suddenly disturbed by her inability to account for small windows of time ever since she had arrived in St. Augustine. What was causing her to feel so spacey?

Eugene seemed unconcerned about the little spells when she described her "time lapses." "Oh, that's normal," he said. "It's just wedding jitters since this is all happening so fast."

She hoped he was right. At any rate, she scarcely had time to think about it; they needed to hurry to the airport to fetch Stephen, after which they would make flower arrangements and attend to a flurry of other last-minute details. For some reason, it was a little frightening to think that she would actually be married in a matter of hours.

33

The Pendulum Speaks

Darla answered the door dressed in a butterfly costume with large, silver wings and bouncing wire antennae decorated with tinsel pom-poms. The wings and antennae looked carelessly incongruous paired with her wrinkled T-shirt and plaid shorts.

"Nice costume," said Gilda.

"Thanks; I like your wig," said Darla. "But just so you know, we aren't handing out our candy yet. In this neighborhood, people usually go trick-or-treating at night—or at least after school—"

"I'm not here for candy, Darla!" Gilda lowered her voice to a whisper. "I'm here because I think I know who the woman in white might be, and I need your help to find out if I'm right."

Darla closed the door behind her and joined Gilda on the porch. "Okay—who is she?"

"Her name is Charlotte Furbo. At least, there's a good reason to think it might be. And she might have been murdered."

"Is this that story where the bride gets yellow fever and is buried alive on her wedding day or something? Because I don't—"

"I'm not talking about that yellow fever ghost story," said

Gilda. "I had a psychic dream about a girl who looked just like the woman in white, and I recognized her from pictures I'd seen of Charlotte. And here's the scary part: In my dream, Charlotte was murdered by her parents—Mr. and Mrs. Furbo."

Darla frowned. "I haven't finished reading that *Master Psychic's Handbook* yet, so I'm not sure how I can help."

"What time do you leave for school?"

"In about half an hour. My mom usually drops me off on her way to the office."

Gilda glanced into Darla's living-room window. "What's your mom doing now?"

"I think she's in the shower."

"We have just enough time to do a quick séance. We have to try to communicate with the woman in white."

"Communicate with her?"

"We need to figure out whether my theory about Charlotte is right. Let's go over to Mr. Pook's house, and—"

"No way. I don't go over to that place—ever." Darla spoke with a certainty that surprised Gilda.

"I thought you'd feel braver now that you have your guardian angel and everything."

"Maybe a little braver. Not dumb-brave."

"Darla, I just slept in that house all night! Are you saying I'm dumb?"

"No, but it sounds like you had a pretty scary dream."

"I'm *glad* I had that dream. It might be the clue we've been looking for."

"I still don't want to go over to Mr. Pook's house—especially to do a séance."

"Then how about here in your house?"

"I guess we can—but we only have a few minutes. And don't tell Mama."

"I won't."

"And if anything really weird happens, we stop."

"Definitely."

Upstairs in Darla's room, Gilda removed a long pearl necklace with a locket pendant from her backpack. "We can use this as a pendulum," she said. She had taken the necklace from a drawer in Eugene's guest room, thinking that one of the antiques from Eugene's Charlotte's Attic business might pick up some vibration in connection with Charlotte.

"It looks like a necklace," said Darla.

"It *is* a necklace, but for today, it's also going to work as our pendulum."

"I read something about pendulums in that book," said Darla. "You swing it back and forth and ask a question."

"Kind of," said Gilda. "But you actually try *not* to swing the pendulum. It's like using a Ouija board. The pendulum will move on its own in response to your questions. You have to try not to force it—and try to be open to either a yes or no answer."

Gilda told Darla to sit across from her on the carpeted floor.

"Wait," said Darla, "let me light my candle before we start." She jumped up, lit her guardian angel candle, and placed it on her dresser. She didn't want to admit it, but the candle made her feel much safer. It was funny how simply deciding to keep a different picture in her mind—the image of her guardian angel—allowed her to slam the door shut on so many of the spirits that often crept into her dreams and thoughts.

"Okay—we need to concentrate on the ghostly woman in white and the name Charlotte Furbo." Gilda held the pendulum in her outstretched hand so that it hung very still. "For me, the pendulum usually swings from side to side if the answer to a question is no. It swings in a circle if the answer is yes. It can be different for different people, though."

Gilda took a deep breath. "First, I'll do a test question." She closed her eyes and concentrated. "Spirit world, please speak to us through this pendulum, and send us the true answers we seek. Is my name Gilda Joyce?"

The pendulum slowly moved in a circle. "Okay, so that definitely shows that a circle means yes," said Gilda.

"We are seeking the truth about Charlotte Furbo," said Gilda. "Charlotte Furbo—are you alive?"

The pendulum moved back and forth.

Darla grabbed Gilda's arm and squeezed. "It's okay, Darla," Gilda whispered. "It's working."

"Are you dead?" Gilda asked.

The pendulum moved in a circle.

"Are you the spirit we have seen—the woman in the white dress?"

The pendulum moved in a circle.

Wow, Gilda thought. *I can't believe how well this is working!* She sometimes had mixed and confusing results with the pendulum, but now it seemed to respond quickly and definitively to her questions.

"Charlotte Furbo: Did Mr. Furbo kill you?" Gilda asked.

The pendulum swung in a circle.

Gilda caught her breath. "Did Mrs. Furbo kill you?" she whispered.

Again the pendulum swung in a circle, now moving even faster. Gilda's heart raced. "I knew it!" she whispered.

"Stop!" Darla suddenly knocked the pendulum from Gilda's hand.

"Hey—why did you do that?"

"Sorry."

"There's nothing to be scared of, Darla. We were getting great answers!"

Darla frowned and shook her head. "It's just—I suddenly *saw* her. I saw the woman in white."

"You *saw* her?"

"Yes—she was only there for a second, but she stood right there in my doorway. There was something on her dress—like a stain."

"A bloodstain?"

"I guess."

"See? That's exactly what I saw in my dream!"

"But she was shaking her head no—telling us we're wrong about something."

Gilda thought for a moment. She was proud of her psychic "little sister" for being brave enough to help with the séance, but she also felt confused. Suddenly, Darla had poked a hole in her theory about what happened to Charlotte. Gilda knew that it was possible to get a "false positive" from reading the pendulum—especially if you had some stake in wanting a yes or no answer. *Did I want the pendulum to confirm my dream more than I realized?* Gilda wondered. "Here," she said, picking up the pendulum and handing it to Darla, "maybe you should take a turn."

"Okay, I guess." Darla held the pendulum the way Gilda showed her. "Charlotte—" she said in a voice as soft as a breeze, "are you here with us in this room?"

The lights flickered. *Yes,* the pendulum answered. Darla caught her breath.

"Go on," Gilda whispered, "ask another question. You're doing great."

"Charlotte—did Mr. Funbo kill you?"

"His name is Mr. Furbo not Mr. Funbo," Gilda interjected.

"Sorry. Did Mr. Furbo kill you?"

The pendulum suddenly swung back and forth very quickly. "NO!" it seemed to shout.

Darla was about to ask another question when the pendulum suddenly flung itself across the room with startling violence. Both girls stared, shocked.

"I guess she doesn't like the pendulum," said Gilda, attempting to lighten the mood, since Darla was obviously shaken by the experience.

"Darla?" Darla's mother knocked on the bedroom door. "What are you up to in there? It's time to leave for school!" Darla's mother opened the door and looked surprised to discover Gilda in her daughter's room. "Oh! Hi, Gilda—great costume! If I didn't know better, I'd think that the two of you were up to some kind of spooky Halloween game."

"I was just tutoring Darla on her spelling," Gilda fibbed.

"But I'd better be going now." She jumped to her feet and adjusted her wig. "Good luck, Darla, and try not to forget that 'i before e' rule I taught you."

"Got it," said Darla, quickly blowing out her guardian angel candle and hiding it under her bed so her mother wouldn't ask questions about it.

As she walked down the path toward Mr. Pook's house, Gilda reflected that although the séance had cast a shadow of doubt over her theory that the Furbos might have murdered their own daughter, it had nevertheless left her all the more certain that Charlotte Furbo was actually dead.

But what makes this mystery so strange and confusing, Gilda thought, *is that we have a ghost without actually having a dead body.* In fact, Charlotte Furbo has never even been reported missing! As far as everyone seems to know, Charlotte is alive and well somewhere in Europe.

So why do Darla and I keep seeing Charlotte's ghost? What is the woman in white trying to tell us?!

34

Ghostwriting

Gilda kicked off her shoes and then headed into the kitchen to get a drink of water. She gazed out the window, reflecting that her mother and Eugene would soon return from picking up Stephen at the airport. This meant that she would probably be forced to help with last-minute wedding preparations rather than focusing on her investigation, which she would strongly prefer.

I can't believe Mom is actually getting married tomorrow morning, Gilda thought. She guessed the rest of her day might be filled with things like arranging flowers and planning hairdos. *Of course, Stephen will find a way to escape the flower arranging in order to go sightseeing around the city,* Gilda thought. *Unless there's some way I can get him interested in this mystery. . . .*

Gilda turned from the kitchen window and caught her breath. Something in the room had changed. An old schoolhouse chalkboard that had previously displayed a list of items to prepare for the wedding now revealed a new cryptic message that had been mysteriously etched in a layer of chalk dust:

LOOK IN THE WELL

Gilda froze. Staring at the message, she felt a prickly sensation on the back of her neck. *Don't panic!* she reminded herself. *Think!* She was certain that the last time she had seen the chalkboard, the wedding list had still been there, written clearly in chalk. Surely her mother and Eugene wouldn't leave a message scrawled with a finger in the dust with no other explanation?

It's a message from a ghost, she thought. But what does it mean?

Look in what well? Where? Eugene had certainly never mentioned anything about a well on the property, had he? *Of course,* Gilda thought, *the old house and its large yard probably contained many secrets.*

To: GILDA JOYCE
From: GILDA JOYCE
RE: MYSTERIOUS MESSAGE—"LOOK IN THE WELL"
To Do:
Determine source of this message. Look outside for evidence
of a well.

Outside Eugene's house, salamanders skittered around Gilda's feet as she hoisted up the heavy petticoats of her Civil War–era costume, pushing through ferns and shuffling along sandy footpaths in search of a well in Eugene's yard.

Do I even know what I'm looking for? Gilda wondered. The truth was, she wasn't at all sure how to look for a well. She knew it would have to be some type of deep hole in the ground, but she was also aware that a very old well might be covered with topsoil and completely hidden from view.

I just hope I don't fall into it out here, she thought. At this thought, Gilda hesitated. *The last thing I need is to be stuck underground in some well.*

Just then Gilda heard the approach of Eugene's car in front of the house. *Stephen's here,* she thought. *Maybe I can get him to help me investigate this.*

It wouldn't be easy to convince Stephen that looking for a well was more important than going to the beach or visiting the Ripley's Believe It Or Not! museum, but she would have to try.

35

Joining Forces

Gilda and Stephen passed through the city gates and walked down St. George Street, where they joined the crowds of people dressed in zany Halloween costumes: sparkly bumblebee antennae, neon-colored makeup, glitter, and wigs, mixed together with the traditional colonial garb of Spanish settlers—capes, knickers, hats, and bonnets.

"So," said Gilda as she attempted to walk without bumping into people with her wide petticoats, "what do you think of our new stepdad?"

"Mr. Pook?" Stephen paused, searching for words. "I don't know. He's okay, I guess." It was Stephen's typical response to subjects that involved uncertainty and troubling emotions—a response that irked Gilda.

"That's all you have to say? Our mom is about to *marry* someone you just met, and all you can say is, 'He's okay'?"

"I like his house. And I like what little I've seen of St. Augustine so far."

"That's a start," said Gilda. "But what did you think of *him*? Were you surprised at all when you saw him at the airport for the first time? I recall feeling just a little bit terrified of his mustache."

"At Mom's age, looks probably don't matter so much."

"Speaking of Mom, did you notice anything different about her?"

"Like what?"

"Like the completely uncharacteristic wardrobe, hair, and makeup she has on today, for starters. And don't even get me started on the new habits she's developed."

"What habits?"

"Eating green jelly at all hours, for one thing."

"At least she isn't smoking. And I thought she looked nice."

Gilda stopped in her tracks. She faced Stephen with hands on hips. "Stephen," she said, "have you ever considered learning a few more words to express yourself? I mean, you can probably squeak by on 'nice' and 'okay' and the occasional 'sweet,' but I think you're limiting your ability to communicate with other humans."

"Okay, now you're starting to drive me crazy. Can't I just walk down the street like a normal person on vacation without overanalyzing everything?"

"No, you can't," Gilda retorted. "We don't have the luxury of being 'normal people on vacation' because our mom is about to get married to a man who lives in a haunted house."

"Here we go." Stephen rolled his eyes.

Gilda tried to explain everything she had experienced during the past couple days: The vision of the ghostly woman in white; the story of Charlotte Furbo and her suspicion that

Charlotte's parents might have murdered their own daughter; the discovery of a possible Indian burial ground on Eugene's property; and finally, the mysterious message, LOOK IN THE WELL.

"So here's my idea, Stephen," Gilda concluded. "I met this girl named Debbie Castle who not only knows a lot about ghosts, but she's also an assistant to a city archaeologist. Anyway, I bet she knows a lot about the history of the old houses around here. If anyone can help us figure out whether there's a well on Eugene's property, she can."

"But, Gilda," said Stephen, "aside from the probable insanity of the whole story you've outlined here, I just heard Mr. Pook telling you that there's no well on the property when you asked him *just a few minutes ago*."

"Right. There's no well that he *knows* about. Or that he's willing to tell me about."

"Why would he keep it a secret?"

"Stephen, Eugene has a human jawbone displayed in his living room, but when I heard him talking with the city archaeologist yesterday, he acted like he had no idea that there might be any bones buried on his property. Mr. Pook is not the most forthcoming guy."

Stephen fell silent for a moment, thinking. "Is that really what that thing is—a jawbone? I thought that was a little weird when I saw it."

"Exactly. He says it's a Timucua Indian bone that was just found on the property."

"I suppose you never know," said Stephen. "If antiques are his business, I can imagine he *might* want to hide some valuable artifacts or bones or something somewhere on the property, like an old well."

"Good thinking, Stephen! A plausible hypothesis!"

Stephen cringed, as if any compliment from Gilda must contain an implicit insult. "But more realistically," he said, "there probably isn't any well if he says there isn't. And besides, I thought we were going to do some sightseeing before all this wedding stuff takes over, not ghost hunting or well hunting or whatever."

They had just reached the ghost tour office, and Gilda caught a glimpse of Debbie Castle sitting at the counter inside, typing on a laptop computer.

"Come on," said Gilda, grabbing Stephen's arm and pulling him toward Debbie's office, "I'll introduce you to Debbie."

Debbie looked up from her computer and smiled when she saw Gilda and Stephen approaching. "Hey, Gilda! Getting ready for the big wedding day tomorrow?"

"Sort of," said Gilda. "We actually wondered if you could help us with something. Oh, and this is my brother, Stephen."

"Nice to meet you. So what can I do for you two?"

"So how scary are these ghost tours?" Stephen asked, piping up.

Gilda stared at her brother, dumbfounded. Then she realized something: Debbie was cute. *Really* cute. *That's why Stephen is suddenly interested in ghosts! Gilda thought. What a doofus!*

"Scary enough!" Debbie replied. "But we don't have any tours running until later this evening. I could give you some tips on haunted places to visit around town in the meantime if you want."

"Actually," said Gilda, elbowing Stephen in the stomach, "we have a question that requires your expertise in both archaeology *and* ghost stories."

"Oh! Even better," said Debbie.

"We've heard that there's a hidden well on Eugene Pook's property," said Gilda, leaning forward and lowering her voice. "And there's a *very* important reason we need to find it."

36

The Secret History

These drawings of the property show that there used to be something right *here*," said Debbie, pointing to an old layout sketch of Eugene's house. "But from the way it's marked, I'm guessing it might be a cistern instead of a well."

"What's a cistern?" Gilda asked.

"It's kind of like a reservoir," said Stephen. "They used them in the old days for catching and storing rainwater."

"Very good, Stephen! A cistern wouldn't be as deep as a well," Debbie explained, "maybe no more than five feet for the houses in St. Augustine. A lot of old houses around here had them as a source of freshwater in the old days."

Debbie, Gilda, and Stephen were huddled around a table in the St. Augustine Historical Society research room—a place that contained all sorts of information on the history of the old city. Within minutes Debbie had located papers documenting the history of Eugene's property from the time it was first built.

"If there is a cistern on the property," Debbie continued, "it's probably lined with the same coquina stone they used to make the fort and the streets in the city." She squinted at the documents. "Of course, these site drawings are very old, and it's obvious that they built a couple additions onto the house since that time. . . . I think that whatever this is may be *underneath* part of the house—which could make it difficult to find."

"She's right," said Stephen. "It looks to me like it's about where Eugene's kitchen is now."

Gilda felt a distinct tickle in her left ear. She remembered the cold spot in the kitchen and the way her mother had stood in the middle of the floor as if she were hypnotized—listening to a ghost. *And that's where I saw the message about the well—in the kitchen,* Gilda thought. "So you're saying they maybe just built the kitchen floor right on top of the old cistern?"

"We can't know without investigating it, but it's possible," said Debbie. "If you ask me, it's a little suspicious that there's no updated documentation of the house's layout after the new addition was built. I mean, in St. Augustine you have to have an archaeologist come out to your house and do a survey of the property before you start tearing down or building just about *anything* in the historic district. And if any artifacts or bones happen to turn up when the digging starts, we have to come out there and document that stuff, too."

"But how can we find out what's down there if it's underneath the house?"

"Simple," said Stephen. "We just pull up Eugene's floorboards."

Suddenly Stephen is an expert on cisterns and carpentry, Gilda thought. *Note to self: the next time I need Stephen's help with something, bring a cute, Southern college girl on board.*

"Do you think we could do that?" said Debbie. By now, she seemed almost as eager as Gilda to explore the property.

"Sure, we could do it," said Stephen. "We would just need a pry bar. The only problem is that we'd have to move the boards carefully so it wouldn't leave a single mark on the floor; otherwise my mother and Eugene would probably disown me."

"I'd get in pretty big trouble, too," Debbie agreed.

"And that's when you'd both tell them that it was all *my* idea," Gilda joked.

"That's big of you," said Stephen, "but I don't think we'd be off the hook that easily."

"Look," said Debbie, "why don't we just go over to Mr. Pook's house and take a look at what we're dealing with? You never know; I might even be able to talk him into helping us uncover the cistern—if there is one. I've managed to convince lots of people that an archaeological excavation isn't such a terrible thing."

"He's pretty stubborn," Gilda warned. "And he might even be hiding something, like some valuable artifacts he doesn't want the archaeologists to know about. Stephen thinks he wants to sell them on the black market."

"I never said *that*," said Stephen.

Debbie sighed with exasperation. "To be honest, I don't think that the things we find under the ground here in St. Augustine can rightly belong to any *one* person considering the hundreds of years of history we've got in this city! But Mr. Pook should know that anything the archaeologists find would still legally belong to him as a property owner; we just need to examine it and document everything. Personally, I think people should donate any artifacts we find on their land to the community, but it's their choice."

"And what if we found human bones?" Gilda asked, thinking of the jawbone in Eugene's display table.

"Human remains are totally different. You don't have any legal right to keep someone else's bones just because you own your house! Even we archaeologists try not to disturb burial sites too much; we just want to know what's down there so we can get a picture of the history."

The three left the research room and made their way back, passing the crowded shops and costumed visitors on St. George Street. "Oh, have you guys been to Tedi's yet?" Debbie pointed to a bustling ice-cream parlor.

"Do you think we might find some clues there?" Gilda asked.

Debbie laughed. "No—I just suddenly have a craving for mint chocolate-chip ice cream. Want to stop in?"

Gilda found a table outside the café while Debbie and Stephen ordered ice cream. She watched them through the window: Stephen was talking about something with gestures that looked more animated than usual. *He's trying to flirt,* Gilda thought. *I bet he's telling her about some archaeology documentary he saw on public television.*

As Debbie handed Gilda a waffle cone stuffed with cookies and cream, peanut-butter cups, and chocolate sprinkles, Gilda's cell phone buzzed with a text message from Wendy:

COULDN'T FIND CHARLOTTE FURBO ONLINE. DID SHE
GET MARRIED? MAYBE A DIFFERENT LAST NAME?? OR
MAYBE YOUR HUNCH IS RIGHT AND SHE IS DECEASED OR
MISSING!!

Gilda quickly typed a message in reply:

THANKS FOR THE HELP! I'M GUESSING DECEASED IS
THE ANSWER! MORE INFO SOON—NOW I'M WATCHING
STEPHEN TRYING TO IMPRESS A GIRL BY TALKING ABOUT
HIS CAR, LOL

As soon as Gilda hit send, she realized her mistake. She could practically feel Wendy's jealousy boiling through her cell phone.

WHAT???! WHO IS THE GIRL?!! AND WHY AREN'T YOU
STOPPING THEM?!

Debbie grinned at Gilda. "Gotta keep up with the gossip back home, huh?"

"Sort of." Gilda glanced down at Wendy's follow-up text:

HELLO???? ARE YOU THERE?????
MORE INFORMATION, PLEASE!!!!!

"Gilda finally figured out how to send text messages last week," Stephen joked.

Gilda was too distracted with crafting an answer to Wendy to bother responding to her brother's dig.

STOP THE HISSY FIT, WENDY! FYI: SHE'S AN ARCHAEOLO-
GIST AND SHE'S HELPING US WITH THE INVESTIGATION.

"Sometimes I hate it when people sit there clicking away on their gadgets while I'm sitting right across from them," Debbie complained. "It's like, pay attention to the person you're actually *with*, you know? Just yesterday I went out on a date with a guy who was texting the entire time. I was like, 'Chill, dude. You're not that important.'"

"That's so annoying," Stephen agreed, trying to look like someone who had no interest in gadgets whatsoever.

SO YOU'RE WILLING TO BREAK MY HEART FOR THE SAKE OF THE INVESTIGATION.

"Excuse me a minute," said Gilda, reading Wendy's last message. "I think I need to make a call."

"Anything wrong?" Debbie asked.

"Just a little fire I need to put out."

Gilda walked around the corner and dialed Wendy's number.

Wendy answered on the first ring. "What does she look like?" she asked.

"Wendy, calm down. She's definitely not interested in Stephen."

"But he's interested in *her.* She's cute, isn't she?"

"She isn't cute. She has huge bifocals and wears support hose with Birkenstock sandals. She has a slight beard."

"I can tell you're making that up."

"Wendy, I shouldn't have said anything about her at all. I actually just thought it was funny."

"Funny?!"

"Stephen's acting like a puppy who wants to lick her face."

"Did they kiss?!"

"Of course not! Look, there's nothing going on here. I mean, seriously nothing. I doubt she's going to ask him to the Sadie Hawkins Day dance, okay?"

"You aren't being a very nice friend right now, you know that?"

"What do you want me to do?"

"I want you to make Stephen like *me*!"

"Well, why didn't you say so? I'll just use my mind-control powers on him right now."

Wendy was unusually silent for a minute. *Is she crying?* Gilda wondered. "Wendy? Are you there?"

"Yes."

"Wendy, Stephen does like you. It's just—sometimes people don't value the things that are right in front of them. Right now he's obsessed with being the big man on campus next year."

"And what about you?"

"What about me?"

"You don't even seem the least bit sad that you might be moving away. I mean, I guess we don't have a beach here in Detroit, but you'd think there'd at least be some loyalty."

"Wendy, I tried to get your parents to adopt me, and you said no way."

"Be serious."

"I am serious. Look, right now I'm just trying to figure out whether Eugene Pook has a secret well on his property."

"A secret well?"

"It's a long story. Remember how I told you I saw a ghost?

Well, a bunch of other weird things have also happened. Just this morning, the girl who lives next door and I tried to do a séance, and right afterward, I discovered a message that said 'Look in the well.'"

"Sounds kind of scary," said Wendy.

Gilda was about to say something dismissive ("I'm a professional, Wendy!"), but then she realized that she agreed. It *was* scary. However, she also realized that she was less frightened by the ghostly message than she was by her mother's looming wedding day. *I guess I've gotten so caught up in thinking about this mystery, I've hardly realized how nervous I really am about getting a new stepdad,* she thought.

But it's really happening. And there's nothing I can do to stop it.

"Gilda?" Wendy prompted. "Are you there?"

"Sorry." Gilda licked her arm. "I've got ice cream dripping down my wrist."

"Remember how my mom would always tell us, 'Micromanage your cones, girls!'?"

Gilda laughed, remembering Mrs. Choy's nonstop directions about the best way to eat ice cream without spilling a drop.

Wendy sighed. "She's such a nut sometimes. Anyway, call me tonight, okay?"

"Definitely," said Gilda. "Oh, and Wendy—"

"What?"

"Put on that Gilda Joyce costume and go out trick-or-treating. You'll feel better."

"You know what? That was actually a really insensitive thing to say."

"Why? I was serious!"

"Well, you happen to know I'm not going out for Halloween if you aren't here."

"Oh. Well—I'm not doing anything fun either, to tell you the truth. I'll be tying bows on roses or lilies and that's about it."

"Good. And don't let Stephen do anything fun either, okay?"

"Definitely not," said Gilda. "He'll be tied to a chair, locked in his room, and having the worst night of his life."

"Good," said Wendy, drily. "That's more like it."

37

What Lies Beneath

The moment Gilda, Stephen, and Debbie walked through Eugene's front door and entered the living room, something strange happened: Lights throughout the house flashed on and off simultaneously.

"Whoa!" Debbie breathed. "Now I see what you mean!"

"You don't even know the half of it," Gilda quipped. "There was one night when a whole dollhouse moved from my room into the hallway all by itself!"

"It might just be an electrical problem—bad wiring or something," said Stephen.

"Maybe," said Debbie. "But in this town, 'bad wiring' is just another way of saying 'old ghosts.'"

The three of them stood silently for a moment, waiting for more signs of ghostly activity or faulty wiring, but there was only an eerie, watchful silence.

"Okay," said Debbie, "I didn't see any signs of a well outside the house, so let's check the interior. Maybe there's something under the floorboards somewhere."

"I think my mom and Eugene are still out picking up the

flowers and vases, but we should hurry," said Gilda. "They could be back any time now."

Debbie stopped in her tracks when she saw the jawbone on display in Eugene's coffee table. "This," she said, pointing, "is a problem."

"Mr. Pook says it's probably a Timucua Indian bone," Gilda explained.

"And it was found on this property?"

"I think so," said Gilda. "Someone may have found it here a long time ago—maybe back when the house was first built."

"I see." Debbie spoke in a clipped, irritated tone. "And I'm sure whoever found it took no notes on where, exactly, it turned up." She pulled out a notebook, jotted some comments, then took a photograph of the bone with her cell-phone camera. "It bugs me so much when people mess up archaeological sites," she fumed. "Is it possible to take this bone out of the case?"

"We don't have time," said Gilda. "What about looking for the well?"

"Okay, okay. But I'd love to take a closer look at that bone to figure out how old it is. That could be some pretty compelling evidence that there's a burial site somewhere on this property."

Debbie walked through the room, examining the floor-boards and the structure of the house. When she walked into the kitchen she stopped in her tracks. "Come here and feel this," she whispered.

Gilda and Stephen followed Debbie into the kitchen. Gilda immediately felt a tingling, cold sensation. She remembered her mother's strange behavior in the kitchen upon their arrival at the house.

"That's a definite cold spot—a sign of spirit activity," said Debbie. "I've had that feeling from time to time on my ghost tour, but it's never been this strong."

"That *is* weird," said Stephen, walking from one side of the room to the other. "It's like walking through an invisible refrigerator."

"Something's up in this room." Debbie walked slowly across the room. "I'd like to look under this floor."

"The thing is," said Stephen, frowning at the floor, "I don't see any way we could pull up these boards without Mom and Eugene finding out."

Debbie reached into her handbag and pulled out a magnifying glass and a small brush. "Some Southern belles carry lipstick and powder; I carry archaeology tools," she joked. "You just never know." She held the magnifying glass over the floorboards and brushed away some dust to get a closer look. "There are some interesting irregularities here in the floor if you look at it closely."

"I doubt we'll have time—" Stephen fell silent because Debbie suddenly reached down and removed an oddly shaped cutting of wood from the floor. It came out easily, and beneath the piece of wood was a handle. "Will you look at that!" said Debbie. "I think we've found something even more interesting than I expected!"

Gilda stared at Debbie with admiration. *Note to self: learn some archaeology and/or carpentry skills for future investigations!*

"Wow," Stephen breathed.

"Looks like a secret trapdoor," said Debbie. The door was an irregular shape, like an enormous jigsaw puzzle piece; if you didn't know it existed, its outline merely looked like natural cracks in the wooden floorboards.

Gilda's heart raced. So there *was* something under the kitchen floor!

"Can you give me a hand, Stephen?" Debbie asked, attempting to pull the handle connected to the trapdoor. "I think it's stuck."

Stephen pulled on the handle until the trapdoor opened slowly, with a creaking sound. The three of them stared, astonished, into a dark cavern beneath the house. In the complete darkness, it was impossible to see what might be hidden there.

"Now hop down in there, Stephen, and check it out," Gilda joked.

"We don't want anyone jumping down there and discovering that it's where Mr. Pook hides his pet alligator or something. . . ." Debbie pulled a flashlight from her bag. Just as she was about to beam it down into the gaping hole, the three of them heard footsteps on the porch outside. "Close it!" Stephen grabbed the trapdoor handle and pushed Gilda out of the way. "They're back!"

"Okay, nobody say anything about this discovery," Gilda whispered. "We'll find another time to investigate it when Mom and Eugene aren't around—maybe later tonight."

Gilda, Debbie, and Stephen managed to close the trapdoor and reseal the wooden floorboards just before Eugene and Mrs. Joyce walked into the house, carrying vases of lilies.

Mom doesn't exactly look like a glowing bride-to-be, Gilda observed. Mrs. Joyce looked thinner and more pale than usual. With dark circles under her eyes, she looked as if she hadn't slept in days.

"Stephen," said Mrs. Joyce, "would you help Eugene carry some things in from the car? We have some bottles of champagne and a few more vases of flowers to bring inside."

"Okay."

Gilda observed Eugene, wondering what the chances were that he didn't know about the trapdoor under his own kitchen. It seemed unlikely. *You lied, Mr. Pook!* she thought. *I bet you knew there was a cistern under the kitchen.* It was all she could do to contain herself from blurting out the accusation right then and there. *But if he is hiding something,* she thought, *I shouldn't tip him off that I know about it until we've had a chance to investigate.*

"Gilda," said Mrs. Joyce wearily, "if you would help me arrange these flowers and the wedding bouquets, that would be wonderful. Oh, and by the way, make sure you get up early tomorrow. Eugene made appointments for both of us to get our hair styled first thing in the morning, before the ceremony."

"No need," said Gilda, "I'll be wearing my 'freaky bridesmaid' wig," said Gilda.

"Not funny, Gilda."

"Okay, but seriously, Mom; I'm planning to wear a hat, so I won't need to have my hair styled."

"Even so, we made an appointment for you."

Should I say something to Mom about finding the cistern under the floor? Gilda wondered. *I can't let her go through with this without at least knowing that Eugene might be hiding something!*

"Can you think of anything else we need to do tomorrow morning, Eugene?" Gilda's mother asked.

"Let's see." Eugene paused to think on his way out the door. "Stephen and I can pick up the cake first thing in the morning while you and Gilda get your hair done. The Furbos are bringing some *hors d'oeuvres* over tomorrow. I think we'll be all set to have the cake and champagne back here at the house after the ceremony."

"Did anyone order the groom's cake?" Gilda asked, mostly to tease Eugene. "I think Mom wanted to surprise you with a cake shaped like a mustache, Mr. Pook."

"Sounds like a surprise I can do without," said Eugene.

"I think that's so cute when people have a groom's cake shaped like one of the groom's hobbies," said Debbie. "I guess Mr. Pook could have something about antiques, right?"

At this comment, Eugene suddenly appeared to notice Debbie's presence in his house. He listened to her suggestion without smiling.

"Or a chocolate graveyard filled with buried skeletons," Gilda blurted. The words slipped out before she could stop herself.

Stephen shook his head with disbelief at Gilda's tactless comment.

Eugene reddened and stalked out of the room. "Back in a minute," he said.

"Way to keep a low profile, Gilda," Stephen muttered.

"Gilda, can you help me cut some of these flower stems and tie bows on the vases?" Mrs. Joyce asked.

"I'd better be going," said Debbie. "Halloween is one of my busiest nights for ghost tours."

"Nice to see you, Debbie," said Mrs. Joyce.

"You too," said Debbie. "I'll see you all tomorrow morning!"

Debbie squeezed Gilda's arm as she passed. "Keep me posted," she whispered as Mrs. Joyce turned to fill a vase with water. "Call me if you find anything important!"

Gilda nodded. "Will do."

"So, Mom," said Gilda as she helped cut flower stems and tie bows around vases, "I noticed you ended up with lilies for the wedding."

"Yes—they're nice."

"But you wanted roses."

"Sometimes it's okay to compromise, Gilda. What's important to me is the marriage."

"And how are you feeling about that part?"

"What part?"

"You're marrying Mr. Pook tomorrow, in case you forgot. Tomorrow you'll become Mrs. Patty-Cakes Pook."

"I'm sure everything will turn out fine."

"You know, Mom, we'd totally understand if you want to cancel this. I mean, we wouldn't hold it against you."

Mrs. Joyce frowned. She gripped a bunch of lilies firmly and trimmed their stems with a large pair of scissors. "Why would you say that, Gilda?"

"Because you don't seem happy. I mean, you don't seem as happy as a person is *supposed* to be right before getting married."

"Honey, even small weddings can be stressful. And just because everything isn't perfect doesn't mean I'm not happy."

"Okay," said Gilda. "But I also just think there's something you should know about Mr. Pook."

"What's that?"

"He might be hiding something."

"We all have secrets, Gilda."

"Yes, but—he might have a *bigger* secret than just getting up in the middle of the night to snack on datil-pepper jelly and ice cream."

"Gilda, please. What are you talking about?"

"Mom," Gilda whispered, "we found a cistern or something under the kitchen floor. But Mr. Pook had told me that there *wasn't* any well on the property!"

"Gilda, you know I don't like you snooping around other people's homes. Anyway, that doesn't mean anything bad. He probably didn't know the well was there. Maybe the previous owners knew about it."

Gilda wondered if her mother had a valid point. What if Eugene honestly didn't know about the cistern?

"You mean this house hasn't always been in Eugene's family?"

"Actually, Eugene said he bought this house from the Furbos. I suppose he was enamored with the house as an antiques storage place even though the relationship with Charlotte didn't work out."

Aha! Gilda thought. *So the Furbos used to own this house! And maybe* they're *the ones who know all about the trapdoor and the old cistern!*

"Mom," said Gilda, "I don't mean to shock you, but there's something else I think you should know."

"What is it, Gilda?"

Gilda decided to just go ahead and blurt out her theory. "I have reason to believe that the Furbos may have murdered their daughter, Charlotte."

Mrs. Joyce ceased arranging flowers and stared at Gilda. "Gilda—that is a horrifying thing to say!"

"I know. But it's an even more horrifying thing to *do*. I can't prove they did it yet, but I just thought you'd want to know what you might be getting into here, Mom. I mean, since Eugene is so close to their family and everything."

Mrs. Joyce began pulling lilies out of the vase she had been arranging, as if she found the flowers offensive in some way. "Gilda, I don't like some of the Furbos' views any more than you do. But making an accusation like that is crossing a line."

"But—"

"I know you like to pursue these little investigations, Gilda, and I also understand that you're angry that I'm marrying someone other than your own father—"

"That has nothing to do with it!"

"I think it has everything to do with it!"

"Mom, I only told you about this because I care about you!"

Mrs. Joyce pulled the entire bunch of lilies from the vase. "If you care about me, then you will let me have my wedding day without ruining it for me—and for everyone else. You're not a little kid, Gilda; it's time to get over these childish games and realize that life changes. People, friendships—even families—they *change* over time!"

Gilda fell silent. Something about her mother's words made her feel as if someone had knocked the wind out of her lungs. She felt tears brimming in her eyes, but she didn't want to cry.

What if Mom is right? she thought. *Is it possible that deep down, I'm trying to find a reason to break up her new marriage because I don't want anything to change—just like the Furbos didn't want anything to change in their family?*

Mrs. Joyce pulled Gilda toward her in an awkward hug. Her mother smelled different—like someone else's perfume. "You know I love you, Gilda," said her mother. "That will never change."

"I know that, Mom," said Gilda. "And I like you, too, sometimes."

"Not love?"

"Okay, I guess I love you, too. Whatever."

"Now—let's finish these arrangements, and then we'll go out for dinner." Mrs. Joyce suddenly spoke in a clipped voice and moved briskly to disguise her frazzled nerves. Secretly, some of Gilda's concerns *had* worried her. *Is Gilda right?* Mrs. Joyce wondered. *Am I less happy than I should be right before my wedding?*

The front door slammed shut and Eugene entered the kitchen followed by Stephen. "So Stephen and I have made our plan for tonight," said Eugene. "We're going out for seafood and then on to a pirate ghost tour on the Matanzas. How does that sound for a Halloween night before the wedding?"

It does sound fun, Gilda had to admit.

"Hey, Stephen," Gilda whispered, pulling her brother aside as Eugene stepped in to oversee the floundering flower-decorating project in the kitchen. "Later tonight, when everyone goes to bed, we'll find out what's down there, underneath the kitchen."

Gilda half expected her brother to protest that there was no way he was getting up in the middle of the night just to open a trapdoor, but to her surprise, he agreed.

"Okay," he said. "I'd actually like to see what's in there, too."

He probably just wants to be able to tell Debbie about it, Gilda thought. *Well, whatever gets him to help is fine with me.*

One way or another, Gilda was determined to find out what was hidden beneath Eugene Pook's house.

38

The Ghost-Pirate

Dear Dad:

I'm feeling a little weird right now.
Maybe I'm nervous because in a few minutes,
I'm going to wake up Stephen, and we'll
tiptoe downstairs with our flashlights and
investigate the contents of that cistern.

Maybe I'm also feeling weird because I
actually had fun tonight when Mom, Eugene,
Stephen, and I all went out on the ghost-
pirate ship together. We were out on the
water, and Captain Jack was telling the
funniest and spookiest pirate tales (Mom
and Eugene liked him so much, they even
reminded him to come to their wedding if
you can believe it!), and the feeling of
being under the stars and looking out
at the lights of St. Augustine from the
dark water and feeling all those spirits
around was kind of magical. I couldn't help
thinking, <u>Maybe</u> <u>we</u> <u>could</u> <u>have</u> <u>more</u> <u>nights</u>

<u>like</u> <u>this,</u> <u>all</u> <u>together.</u> I mean, what if
Stephen and I just never looked down in
the cistern? What if I just <u>pretend</u> that
I never suspected any dark secrets? If I
pretend not to see ghosts, like Darla has
done for years, will they eventually go
away? Would I stop seeing the woman in
white? Would I stop having nightmares about
Charlotte's death?

But you know me, Dad. I can't pretend
that I DON'T know what I DO know.

Besides, I can't miss this golden
opportunity to wake Stephen from his beauty
sleep in the middle of the night.

Wish me luck, Dad, and if you're out
there, please protect me from any evil
spirits that might be lurking around this
house!

Love,

Gilda

39

The Secret in the Cistern

I can't believe I agreed to do this," Stephen whispered. He and Gilda tiptoed down the hallway, doing their best to avoid stepping on the creaky spots in the floor. The glow of Gilda's flashlight made the antique furniture and artifacts in the house look spooky and strange.

"You know you want to see what's in there just as much as I do," Gilda replied.

"Still—I can't believe I'm doing this."

"It's probably the most fun you've ever had on Halloween."

"That might actually be true."

They made their way down the long staircase, then walked through the living room. Gilda held her breath as she inched silently past the coffee table that contained the jawbone.

They froze at the sound of something creaking in the next room.

"Did you hear that?" Gilda whispered.

"No."

Gilda cautiously moved toward the dining room and kitchen.

"Let's hurry up if we're doing this, Gilda," Stephen

snapped. "There aren't any ghosts down here, if that's what you're worried about."

"You sure about that, son?"

Gilda and Stephen gasped. A light shone directly in their eyes, and for a moment, they could only make out a shadowy figure who was pointing a flashlight at them. Then Gilda realized that it was Eugene. He had been sitting there, alone in the darkness.

Was he waiting for us? Gilda wondered. *Did Mom say something to him after I told her about the cistern? And why is he sitting there in the dark, with only a flashlight?*

"I couldn't sleep," said Eugene. "Must be wedding jitters."

"We couldn't sleep either," said Gilda, trying to disguise the panic in her voice.

"So you thought you'd take a little nighttime walk?" Eugene was obviously suspicious.

"I was actually just coming down to get a drink of water," said Stephen. "I'll be getting back to bed."

"Have a seat, both of you," said Eugene, pulling out a chair from the dining table and pointing to it. Something about his tone made them obey him. Eugene lit his antique lantern, and as Gilda's eyes adjusted to the dim light, she saw that Eugene had an assortment of objects in front of him, including two old rifles. There were also small bottles of cleaning fluids, an assortment of brushes of different sizes, and some other small antiques, including an old photograph.

"Sometimes when I can't sleep I get up and clean my antiques," said Eugene. "It relaxes me."

Gilda and Stephen nodded, both now wishing that they could simply retreat from the room and go back to bed.

"See this gun? It's beautifully carved. Just look at that craftsmanship. It was Bob Furbo who gave me this gun. He taught me everything I know about antique rifles—how to take care of them."

For a moment Gilda was terrified that Eugene had lost his wits and might actually be planning to use one of the guns, but then she realized that he was getting ready to tell a story.

"My daddy came down to St. Augustine to work on the railroad," said Eugene. "He and Mama were from up in Louisiana. I didn't have any deep roots here in St. Augustine like some folks do, you know. We was always 'them folks from Louisiana.'"

Gilda wondered where Eugene was heading with all of this. He seemed to be in a strangely confessional mood, and while Gilda was usually the first to want to hear intriguing stories, sitting in the darkness with guns on the table made for an uncomfortable discussion.

"I don't know if I told you this," Eugene continued, "but one morning, I watched my daddy get on the train at the St. Augustine station, and he never did come back. After that, I was known as 'that boy whose daddy took off on the train.'

"We didn't have much money, and Mama never did work. You know what she did for money instead of working?"

Gilda and Stephen both shook their heads. They stared at Eugene, transfixed and disturbed by this tale.

"She sold things. Every cotton-pickin' thing she and Daddy had brought from Louisiana, Mama sold. Furniture, paintings, silver, jewelry, clothing." He enumerated the items on his fingers. "Everything.

"Well, there were a handful of things that she did not sell only because I hid them from her. And this—this is one of them." Eugene handed Gilda a small tintype photograph in an antique silver frame. "That's my grandma," he said, pointing. "That was taken when she was young."

The tiny picture struck Gilda as unusual for its time because Eugene's grandmother was photographed with her hair long and loose instead of pulled into a severe updo. A faint, inscrutable smile played upon her lips. She looked angelic, with her soft, powdered skin and the romantic waves of her hair.

Then Gilda realized something else about the photograph: *She looks like Charlotte,* she thought.

"Whenever I looked at this photograph, I felt peaceful," said Eugene. "I felt almost like my grandma was still with me.

"You see, when I was a boy, I realized that most people were very unreliable. But objects like this photograph—if you knew how to take care of them, you could keep some of them around forever, and they wouldn't change. I guess maybe that's when I got interested in antiques.

"As soon as I was old enough, I got a job working in an antiques shop. I loved how some old things could actually become more valuable over time *if* you took care of 'em. And you know—the more I studied the value of antiques, and the more I built my collection by going to all the big auctions and estate sales, the more I got to know some of the oldest families in this community. They became my customers. And do you know, for the first time in my life, I had their respect. They respected me because I knew even more about these objects than they did. They saw that I understood their past and what they wanted to preserve. I guess I always liked that about some of the old-timers: How rooted they were to a single place . . . how well they knew this old city.

"When Mama died, I sold that empty old house of hers and used all my savings to purchase my own shop on Antiques Row in the city." Eugene paused for a moment, as if watching a movie of his memory amidst the shadows cast on the wall by the lantern light. "And that's where I met Charlotte. But you probably don't want to hear about that."

"Oh, we *definitely* want to hear about that," said Gilda, her curiosity now outweighing her discomfort.

Stephen kicked her under the table, obviously wanting to extract himself from the whole conversation.

"I'll never forget the day I met Charlotte, because when she walked into my shop, she was dressed head to toe in vintage clothes. For a second I actually thought I was seeing a ghost. She almost looked like someone who stepped out of another time in history. Except for her long hair, she looked like one of those flappers from the nineteen twenties during the Gilded Age here in St. Augustine.

"Well, I quickly found out that she was from one of the old Minorcan families and that she happened to know even more about the things in my shop than I did. She had grown up with beautiful furniture and china all around her. I learned a lot from Charlotte. In fact, a lot of the clothes and furniture still in this house are things that belonged to her."

I bet that dress I wore to the wedding rehearsal belonged to Charlotte, Gilda thought. *Maybe that's part of the reason I was able to see her ghost!*

"Yes, there are *many* valuable things in this house," said Eugene, looking at Gilda and Stephen with a strange intensity. "And, as you've probably guessed, this house has some secrets."

Gilda and Stephen sat very still, frozen with anticipation. *What is he going to tell us?* Gilda wondered.

"You're family now," said Eugene, "so I think it's time that I shared the secret with you." He looked at them both.

Gilda nodded as if hypnotized. "Yes," she whispered. "We want to know."

Eugene nodded. "Good. Then follow me."

Gilda and Stephen looked at each other, and Stephen shrugged as if to say, Don't ask *me* what to do!

Carrying the lantern, Eugene walked into the kitchen. Again, Gilda felt a draft of cold air that seemed to rise up from the floor.

Eugene crouched down and felt with his hand along the floor. "Here—I think this is it." He carefully lifted the large puzzle piece of wood from the floor and located the secret handle. Then, with a grunt, he pulled open the trapdoor to reveal the dark pit below.

"You don't seem surprised," he said, looking at Gilda and Stephen with undisguised suspicion.

"Oh, we're just speechless," said Gilda.

"Yeah," said Stephen. "That is really weird."

"Follow me down," said Eugene, "and I'll show you where a pirate hides his treasure."

Something about this comment gave Gilda the creeps. She knew it was highly unlikely that Eugene was about to reveal a treasure chest filled with gold coins and jewels. *So what is he planning to show us?* she wondered. She fought an urge to grab a corner of Stephen's T-shirt and cling to it like a security blanket as she followed him toward the cistern.

A short ladder leaned against the wall closest to the trapdoor. Eugene climbed down and then crouched below, peering up at them from the darkness, holding his lantern. Gilda and Stephen followed him down into the cistern.

The cistern smelled damp and faintly rusty. Crouching in the claustrophobic space, Gilda felt the clammy air and the rough coquina stones under her bare feet. She thought of her dream of the yellow fever cemetery but tried to push the image from her mind.

Gilda spied a long bench covered in white cloth and an antique jewelry box that looked hand-painted. Was Eugene going to show them something hidden in the jewelry box?

"Now," said Eugene, "it's time for these games to end." His face looked macabre in the lamplight.

"What do you mean?" Gilda whispered.

"You asked about a well, Gilda. And I'm guessing that the appearance of Miss Debbie Castle on my property was not exactly a coincidence. I have reason to believe that you already knew about this cistern."

"We guessed there *might* be something here," said Stephen, "but we weren't sure."

"I see," said Eugene, leaning toward the two of them. "And what else did you think *might* be down here?"

"We had no idea," said Gilda. "We were just curious."

"And we don't *need* to know anything," said Stephen hastily.

"Did you ever hear the saying, 'Curiosity killed the cat'?"

Gilda nodded. She felt scared, but also strangely transfixed. She still desperately wanted to know what Eugene was hiding.

"Look," said Stephen, "we don't need to know any secrets. We'll just go back up to bed now."

"Oh, no," said Eugene. "Like I said, you're both family now. And let's be honest: Now that you know about my hiding place for my most valuable treasure, you'll want to explore it soon enough. So here." He handed Gilda a key. "Explore it."

"What's this key for?"

"I'm sure you'll figure that out. Oh, but we'll need a bit more light first. Let me grab another lantern or a flashlight from the kitchen."

Eugene swiftly climbed the ladder out of the cistern. As Gilda moved her flashlight around in the darkness, she walked over to the bench and lifted the white cloth.

Gilda gasped with surprise: "Stephen—look!"

It wasn't a bench at all; *it was a sealed coffin.*

A dried bouquet of lilies rested on top of the coffin—*a bridal bouquet.* Gilda saw that a rough inscription had been laboriously carved by hand into the top of the casket:

To my Charlotte—

I loved you too briefly
Seemed only a day;
I'll love you forever
For here you will stay.
No more shall you wander
No more shall you roam;
For you're glued to my heart
And I'm chained to your bones.

Gilda also noticed something soft and white propped against the base of the coffin—a couple of pillows and a blanket. An image flashed in her mind: Eugene tiptoeing downstairs in the middle of the night to rest his head against the coffin.

Stunned and speechless, Gilda turned around just in time to see the ladder swiftly disappear from the cistern before the trapdoor slammed shut over their heads.

40

The Key

Hey! Let us out!" Gilda and Stephen pounded on the trapdoor, but the only response was the sound of a latch clicking shut and something that sounded like a heavy piece of furniture being moved.

"He's weighing down the trapdoor so we can't get out," said Stephen.

Stephen examined the boards overhead, looking for a weak spot. Groaning with the effort, he pressed up on the trapdoor with his hands. He tried punching the trapdoor from beneath, but only succeeded in injuring his hand. "Ow!"

"Maybe if we create a big disturbance, Mom will hear us and come downstairs," Gilda suggested. Both she and Stephen yelled at the top of their lungs: *"HELP! HELP! HEEEEEELP! MOM! HELP!"*

But nobody came to help them. "I think it's pretty difficult to hear anything from upstairs," said Gilda, pausing to catch her breath. *It wouldn't be very hard for Eugene to simply keep Mom out of the kitchen until the wedding,* she thought, feeling queasy at the full implications of being trapped underground with a coffin containing a dead body. *And who knows what he's planning to do with us.* Her thoughts raced as she struggled to control her urge to break into hysterical tears. More than anything, she wanted to get out of that dark, clammy cistern.

"Wait a minute," said Stephen. "Do you think he might be playing a big joke on us?" He kicked the coffin. "I mean, it's Halloween. Maybe that thing is fake. Or empty."

"It *isn't* fake," said Gilda. "For one thing, Mr. Pook has a terrible sense of humor."

"Exactly my point," said Stephen. "Although I suppose carving a bad poem into a coffin is a lot of trouble to go to just to make a joke on Halloween night."

Gilda shone her flashlight over the top of the casket. Large nails sealed the rough-hewn coffin shut. "*He's* the one who did it," Gilda said. "Eugene killed Charlotte Furbo. That's why he locked us down here; he knew that we were about to figure it out for ourselves."

Why didn't I figure it out sooner? Gilda wondered. Somehow she hadn't wanted to consider the real possibility that Eugene might be a murderer. True, she found him unlikable, but she also felt sympathy for the little boy who had lost his father at the train station. And she had had fun with him and her mom on the pirate ship, too. *Maybe, deep down, part of me hoped that it really would work out—not just for Mom, but for all of us,* she thought.

"If Eugene is really a murderer, Gilda, then we're in deep, deep trouble, because there's not much incentive for him to keep us alive," said Stephen. "I mean, if he really did kill this woman and now we have proof, he's not going to want us around to tell the tale."

No, Gilda thought. *My life cannot end in this dank old cistern, underneath Mr. Pook's house!* There had to be some way out of this mess. "Well," she said, "what is Mr. Pook going to tell everyone when we don't show up at the wedding?"

"He could blame it on *us*. He'll say we ran away or something. Then maybe they'll file a missing-person report and look everywhere for us. But by the time they suspect Eugene, he will have had plenty of time to get rid of us—or he could just let us run out of air down here."

"Sort of like what he did to Charlotte," Gilda whispered. *So* that's *what happened,* Gilda thought. *Eugene killed Charlotte, and then simply told everyone that she ran off to Europe and left him.*

"I just want to say one thing," said Stephen, placing his hands on Gilda's shoulders. "Thank you so much for the best Halloween I've ever had."

"Hey, I'm not the one who locked us in here!" Gilda knew that Stephen's sarcastic comment was partly an attempt to disguise his own rising panic at their plight, but her temper flared nevertheless.

"But it was *your* idea to go down and investigate the cistern in the middle of the night. If I hadn't listened to you, I'd still be sleeping soundly in my bed."

"Then maybe you should blame your own lack of judgment instead of blaming your little sister," Gilda snapped. "And besides, you're forgetting about Mom! If we hadn't come down here, we never would have known that she's about to marry a killer!" The thought nauseated Gilda. *Will our whole family end up down here trapped in the cistern together?!*

"Believe me, Gilda, the thought crossed my mind. But it's not as if we can do anything to stop Mom while we're stuck down here!" Sighing, Stephen crouched on the floor and leaned his back against the rough stone wall. "Look—I'm sorry I blamed you; this isn't your fault. We shouldn't waste oxygen with all this arguing, anyway."

"How much oxygen do you think we have down here?" With the trapdoor closed, the air already felt heavy and stale.

"I have no idea."

"Can't you estimate? I mean, you're the mathematician and engineer."

"But not a biologist. I'd just be guessing."

"Maybe we should both try breathing with one nostril."

"It's a shame nobody else is around to hear these last little witticisms, Gilda."

"Okay, we're two smart people, Stephen. We have to literally think outside the box and find a way out of here. Like—maybe there's some kind of machine you could make with wood if we broke apart that coffin. Maybe we could force our way out!"

"First of all, we don't have any tools down here to pry open a coffin. Second of all, ARE YOU CRAZY? I don't exactly want to spend whatever time I have left down here smelling some corpse that's been down here for who-knows-how-long!"

"At least I'm trying to come up with a solution." Gilda ran her fingers over the rough stones. *Send me an idea, send me an idea. . . .*

"I've got it!" said Gilda.

"What?"

"Debbie Castle! She knows about the cistern. And thanks to me, she and her mother were invited to the wedding. So when the two of us don't show up for the ceremony, she'll suspect something. At least she'll know where to look! Otherwise it could take years to figure out that we're down here."

"Good point," said Stephen, a more positive note entering his voice. "But let's just hope she'd actually think of looking here *soon* enough. I mean, if Eugene comes up with some convincing lie, she won't be very likely to just take off from the wedding ceremony, break into his kitchen, and start pulling open the trapdoor without his permission."

Gilda realized she had been turning the key Eugene had given her over and over in her sweaty hand. "I wonder what this key is for?"

"There's no keyhole on the trapdoor; I already checked."

Gilda shone her flashlight on the jewelry box that had been on top of the coffin and saw a keyhole in front. *Does he keep some of Charlotte's most valuable jewelry in here?* she wondered as she fit the key into the keyhole and opened the box.

Inside, she discovered something that lifted her spirits, even if it did nothing to solve her immediate problem.

The box contained a small, leather-bound diary and some yellowed stationery. "Look, Stephen! I found Charlotte's diary!"

"How does that help us?"

"I guess it doesn't." Nevertheless, Gilda felt excited to

read the journal despite the dire circumstances in which she found herself. She flipped through Charlotte's diary entries, skimming writings about dances, favorite dresses, tea parties, and artistic displays she wanted to create for Charlotte's Attic. She read entries about the repeated engagement proposals and gifts from a "handsome" but "awkward" older gentleman named Mr. Eugene Pook. *Maybe now I'll finally understand who the woman in white really was,* Gilda thought as she pored over the entries.

41

Charlotte's Diary

Dear Diary:
Chance, Chance, Chance, Chance
Chance Owens
Mrs. Charlotte Owens
Mrs. Charlotte Pook
Mrs. Eugene Pook
Mrs. Charlotte Owens
Mrs. Chance Owens

Something wonderful and terrible has happened—I've fallen in love.

It's terrible because I'm engaged to be married to Eugene Pook, but wonderful because I've fallen in love with Chance Owens.

I met him today at the barbecue festival in the Old City. We danced to the blues, and we talked about absolutely everything, and, as we danced, I knew we were soul mates whose HEARTS recognized each other. Either I'm in love or I've gone crazy. I don't know which! All I know is that I want to escape with him to somewhere far away—to a whole unexplored world. Maybe this is what my great-great-great-grandparents felt hundreds of years ago when they left the port of Minorca for Florida. I reckon there were a few of them who just longed to get on a boat and travel far away from all the people they knew. I wonder how hard it was for them to leave behind everything they knew and loved back then?

Some people stared at me and Chance, but I was so happy at that moment, I didn't give a hoot. I wonder if Mama and Daddy will hear about it. They would be so angry with me. They shouldn't be. Chance comes from a St. Augustine family of doctors, teachers, musicians, and barbecue experts—a family as old and proud as ours, if you think about it! But Chance and I are from different sides of the same world.

"My parents live in a house that Martin Luther King once visited," Chance said, "and your daddy marched in parades with the Ku Klux Klan. That's the difference between the two of us."

Chance is in the army, and as we walked through the Mission after the dance, he told me that he's going to be stationed overseas in Europe.

"You could come with me," he told me. "Anything is possible; we have choices."

"Chance," I said, "my mama and daddy would probably disown me. Besides, I'm supposed to get married right here in a few days."

He laughed when I said that. "You don't seem like someone who's about to get married," he said.

I'm scared he's right, because it felt so natural to just lean my head on his shoulder, and I liked the way he touched my hair as we looked at the stars over the bay. It felt like we were already a couple.

"Think about it," he said. "We're young. There's a whole world out there to explore; we've got our whole lives ahead of us."

I so want to GO with him! But I'm afraid of what would happen. And poor Eugene! I do care about him, and I don't want to break his poor old heart. It wasn't so long ago that I was excited to start our new business, Charlotte's Attic, and make all those precious displays for our store. And I loved how easy it was to make Mama and Daddy so happy with the wedding planning— talking about the food, the cake, trying on Mama's silk wedding gown, the flowers and all. . . . Why can't I have all of that with Chance?

Dear Chance,
I want to run away and leave everything I know behind.
But I'm terrified to go!
But when I think of my whole life married to Eugene
I feel I'm being buried alive.
"You know where to find me," you said, "if you
change your mind."
But Chance, Chance, Chance, Chance,
why didn't your good luck happen to me
in time?

Dear Diary,

It's Halloween Night, and I'm sitting in Daddy's truck with the window open. A cloud just spit a big ole drop on my arm and it's probably going to pour down rain any minute.

I hope it's lucky rain.

The wedding is supposed to be tomorrow morning, but I won't be there. Nobody will be there, because I just told Mama and Daddy that I can't marry Eugene.

I've never seen Mama and Daddy look at me like that—like their faces were two blocks of flat stone.

"Oh, you've just got cold feet," Mama said. "It's wedding jitters."

We were doing a last fitting of my wedding dress—the dress Mama wore when she got married—and Mama was adjusting one of the shoulder straps.

I'm still wearing the wedding dress now. Rain is falling on it, but it doesn't matter because I won't be wearing it in any ceremony.

"No, Mama," I said. "It isn't just wedding jitters."

"What, then?"

How could I explain how I felt today at the wedding rehearsal—like there wasn't enough oxygen in the air? How could I explain how, just last night, I had another dream that I was sick from yellow fever and buried alive in the Huguenot Cemetery, and in the dream the wooden coffin turned into Eugene, who was holding me down and suffocating me underground?

So I just told them the simple truth. "Because I love someone else," I said. And then I told them who.

Once I said it, I realized I was free. I don't have to marry Eugene, I realized. It's my life and my decision. It was so simple, like waking up and seeing the sunlight after a long, long nightmare.

I knew there would be tears, and I knew Daddy would yell, but I guess I didn't really expect Mama and Daddy to tell me to get out. Can you imagine?! Their own daughter!

"The truth will set you free."

I pray that it's true.

But I'm not free yet, because I haven't told Eugene the truth. He's so happy right now; he was just beaming tonight when Daddy gave him his wedding gift—an antique rifle. "I'll teach you to use it," said Daddy. "We'll go skeet shooting together next week."

Well, Eugene's cheeks got so pink and happy—he looked like a little boy on his birthday.

And that's when I realized something else—that Eugene wants to marry my family more than he wants to marry me. Come to think of it, Mama and Daddy and I disagree on most everything, and Eugene always takes their side over mine. It's like he's more interested in what he calls "the authentic Florida heritage" than some of the real Minorcan people, like me.

If I could leave without telling him, I almost think I would. But I have to face him: it would be even more hurtful to let him show up in his tuxedo tomorrow morning all hopeful and happy, only to hear the news from Mama and Daddy.

I have this song in my mind that my friends and I used to sing when we were jumping rope back when we were small:

Lucky rain,
Lucky rain,
RAIN ON ME!
Lucky rain,
Lucky rain,
SET ME FREE!

42

The Lie

But it isn't like them to decide they just aren't showing up!"
Mrs. Joyce frowned at the letter Eugene had presented to her.
She sat in the beauty parlor with her auburn hair swept back in
a French twist. A manicurist painted her fingernails with pink
polish as she scrutinized the letter for the third time:

```
Dear Mama and Eugene:
Steven and I went out ghost
hunting early this morning, and we
are not going to the wedding. Sorry
to disappoint you, but we realized we
have some sightseeing to do. Plus,
since I didn't get to be the wedding
planner, the wedding is no fun. I also
never enjoyed them datil peppers of
Mr. Pook's and I reckon they will be
everywhere at the reception.
    Your daughter,
    Gilda
```

Eugene had hastily typed the note on Gilda's old typewriter, hoping that this ruse would at least buy him some time until he figured out what—if anything—he would do with Gilda and Stephen.

"There's something very strange about this letter!" Mrs. Joyce squinted at the words. "It looks like the sort of note Gilda would write on her typewriter," she said, "but there's something odd about it. I can't explain why, but it doesn't really *sound* like her!" Mrs. Joyce reread the letter with a concerned expression, her hand covering her mouth. "Do you think they got into some kind of trouble last night?" She looked up at Eugene. "I'm wondering if they did something stupid like sneaking some of the wedding champagne. Gilda actually spelled Stephen's name wrong here!"

"They're teenagers," said Eugene. "We knew this wedding might be pretty upsetting for them, so maybe this is their way of coping. Besides, Gilda loves that ghost-hunting stuff. She probably couldn't resist on Halloween."

"Yes—but not showing up for the wedding?!" Mrs. Joyce remembered the argument she and Gilda had had the day before and the doubts Gilda had expressed. Had Gilda actually been so angry she was willing to skip the entire ceremony and convince Stephen to do the same?

"Believe me, I've heard of kids doing worse," said Eugene. "You know, I thought I heard them sneak out the door early this morning. . . . I just wish I had gotten up to talk to them."

"Well, I can't very well get married without my children there for the ceremony!"

Eugene realized he had backed himself into a very tight corner. "Patty," he said, standing behind Mrs. Joyce and speaking to her reflection in the mirror, "just take a look at yourself. You look beautiful. See how that diamond ring shines on your finger! This is *our* day. It's a small wedding anyway—small and perfect. Really, the only two people who need to be there at all are you and me."

Mrs. Joyce looked in the mirror and saw that Eugene was right. With her hair, makeup, and dress complete, she had been transformed—younger and more beautiful than she had looked in years. And there was Eugene—his reflection so hopeful—almost pleading as he stood next to her. "This is the happiest day of my life," he said, gazing at Mrs. Joyce's reflection. "And I have something very special for you to wear to the wedding."

Eugene gave her a small box and she opened it. Inside, she found a pearl necklace.

"It belonged to my grandmother," said Eugene. "And I want you to have it."

The manicurist shook her head. "So, so sweet!" she murmured. "I wish I had a husband like you, Mr. Pook!"

Eugene chuckled. "There," he said, helping Mrs. Joyce adjust the clasp of the necklace.

"Thank you, Eugene. It's lovely. But I——"

"Now—don't you worry about Gilda and Stephen. I reckon they'll have a change of heart and turn up for the wedding at the last minute. Why let a teenage mistake spoil our whole day after all these preparations?"

"I suppose," said Mrs. Joyce, more because she couldn't imagine disappointing everyone—the priest, the musicians, the Furbos, the friends Gilda invited—than because she actually agreed. *But I'm going to kill Gilda and Stephen when I see them!* she thought.

43

The Wedding Specter

Darla and her mother were the first guests to arrive for the wedding; the musicians were just sitting down to begin their prelude music. As the soft sounds of guitar and harp filled the air, Darla observed Mrs. Joyce and Eugene as they stood nearby, speaking earnestly with the priest.

Where is Gilda? Darla wondered. It seemed strange that she and her brother hadn't arrived yet.

An elderly couple named the Furbos arrived and said hello to Darla's mother. Darla scrutinized their suntanned, wrinkled faces as she recalled Gilda's theory: *"I think the Furbos killed Charlotte."*

Darla felt very suddenly unwell. A weight pressed down upon her chest and she felt as if there wasn't quite enough air to breathe, even though a gentle breeze was blowing off the bay. It was a feeling that she recognized all too well—the sense that someone was staring at her intensely—someone that nobody else could see.

Think about your guardian angel, Darla reminded herself. *No spirits can touch you unless you invite them in.*

Turning to glance behind, Darla saw exactly what she

feared: *The woman in white stood watching her from a short distance away*. Clearly, nobody else saw the ghostly bride wearing a bloodstained wedding gown. Nobody else saw Charlotte's ghost. Darla quickly faced forward in her seat, not wanting to see the vision. *Gilda would tell me to make contact with her—to try to find out what she wants,* Darla told herself. But without Gilda there, she felt too terrified to think like an investigator. She hadn't forgotten the day when this same ghost led her into Mr. Pook's house—to the vision that traumatized her for years afterward.

Darla opened her purse and pulled out her cell phone. With any luck there would be some text messages to distract her. But before she could check her in-box, her mother grabbed her wrist.

"Not at a wedding!" Mary Louise hissed.

Now the weight on Darla's chest felt heavier—the air thicker. *Calm down,* she told herself. *Don't panic!* She took deep breaths and placed her elbows on her knees, struggling to gain control of her breathing.

Suddenly a strange picture entered Darla's mind—an image of Gilda trapped inside a box, deep beneath the ground. A place with no air. *Something happened to Gilda in Mr. Pook's house,* Darla realized. *She's in danger.*

Help! the woman in white seemed to whisper to her. *Help!*

Darla turned around. Charlotte's ghost was still there, and she was pointing toward something she wanted Darla to see.

She's pointing in the direction of Mr. Pook's house, Darla thought.

Follow me, the ghost seemed to say. *Hurry!*

It would only take her a few minutes to get to Mr. Pook's

house if she ran. "Mom," Darla whispered breathlessly, "I'll be back in a minute."

"Wait! Where are you going?"

"I forgot I'm supposed to help Gilda with something before the wedding!"

Before her mother could stop her, Darla raced across the grass, toward Mr. Pook's house on Water Street.

44

Feats of Strength

When Darla reached Mr. Pook's house, she stood frozen on the sidewalk outside his garden gate. The memory of skeletons moving inside the house paralyzed her.

Help. The ghost did not speak the word, but Darla somehow heard it in her mind. *HELP.* Again she saw the image of Gilda trapped inside the house.

Feeling as if she were walking into a burning building, Darla took a deep breath and forced herself to walk up the path, across the front porch, and through the unlocked front door.

Inside, the house was silent. The only sound was the *tick, tock* of the grandfather clock. *Guardian angel, please protect me,* Darla whispered to herself as she glimpsed her reflection in the eye-shaped mirror upon the wall. So far, so good. No bones wriggling on the floor. But she had the terrible feeling that something might jump out at her at any moment.

Suddenly Darla saw a bright spot floating just above the kitchen floor—an orb that gradually took the shape of the woman in white. As she drew closer, Darla saw the bright purple-red flower that decorated her white gown—a flower that turned into a bloodstain.

The ghost pointed to the words etched in dust on a chalkboard:

LOOK UNDER THE FLOOR

"But how can I look under the floor?" Darla asked aloud.

"Hello?" a weak, muffled voice came from under the floor-boards.

Darla caught her breath. "Who's there?" Her voice came out as a squeak.

"Hey! Is somebody up there?"

It was Gilda's voice. Darla exhaled, feeling relieved. "Gilda! It's me—Darla! Where are you?"

"We're down here—just hanging out under the kitchen."

"What are you doing down there?"

"It's nice down here if you don't like breathing."

"Hey!" It was a teenage boy's voice. "Can you get us out of here? We're running out of air!"

"How do I get you out?"

"I'll knock on the floor where the trapdoor is," said Stephen. "Hear that? It's hard to see where you need to lift, but you just have to use your fingernails to pry up a piece of wood, and then there's a hidden handle."

Darla struggled to quell a rising sense of panic as she thought of Gilda and her brother running out of air. "There's a problem here," she said, "a big armoire is in the middle of the floor—probably right over the trapdoor. I'm not sure I can move it."

Down in the cistern, Stephen covered his face in his hands. "I forgot about that," he said glumly. "She'll never be able to move it by herself."

Darla pressed her palms against the heavy armoire that Eugene had dragged over the trapdoor. She leaned all her weight against it, but it scarcely budged.

"I think I need to go back and get some help!" Darla shouted. *What if I can't open it in time?!* she worried. "I'm not very good at stuff like this . . ."

But as Darla attempted to lean against the armoire once more, she sensed that she was not alone. She now felt as if the woman in white, the broken soldiers, the Indian villagers—all the ghosts of the house were there by her side to help her. She did not fear them; she told herself that these were the spirits of ancestors who had come to her side to help her because only she could see and hear them. With the strength of several poltergeists, Darla gave the armoire a final shove and it miraculously moved across the room.

Moving her hands across the floor, Darla carefully searched for the piece of irregular wood that concealed the cistern.

A long, anxious minute later, she peered down into the darkness. She saw Gilda and Stephen huddled together, leaning against one of the coquina stone walls. Exhausted and partly hidden in the darkness, they looked very small to her—more like young, frightened children than teenagers—as they shielded their eyes from the sudden light.

"Thank God," said Stephen, rising to his feet and taking in deep, relieved breaths of air.

"Totally awesome job, Darla!" Gilda declared, her voice a hoarse croak. Her brave words belied the exhausted tears that rolled down her cheeks.

45

The Grand Entrance

The problem," said the priest, "is that we've got another wedding scheduled right after yours. I'm sorry, but we can't wait any longer."

Mrs. Joyce scanned her surroundings, looking for some sign of Gilda and Stephen.

"It's okay, Patty." Eugene put his arm around her protectively. Finally he was having the wedding day he should have had twenty years ago. *This time, nothing is going to spoil it,* he told himself. *This time, I'm in control.*

The guitarist shot the priest an impatient look. The musicians had finished their repertoire of prelude music and had begun repeating the same pieces.

Shifting in their seats, the sparse group of guests observed the wedding couple with growing anticipation.

"Someone's got cold feet," Mrs. Furbo muttered.

"I *told* him, 'Don't pick another one like Charlotte,'" Mr. Furbo said.

Sitting behind the Furbos, Captain Jack extended his legs and arms in a giant stretch, and then folded his arms across his chest as if preparing for a nap in the sun. He had slightly altered his pirate attire for the occasion of the wedding, choosing a clean T-shirt instead of the gold necklaces and sleeveless, torn shirts that revealed his shoulder-to-wrist tattoos.

As he gazed out at the bay, something very interesting caught his attention: The same gopher tortoise he had spotted a couple days ago lumbered slowly toward the wedding party, pausing to chew blades of grass along the way. Captain Jack observed the animal with a sleepy smile.

Mrs. Furbo also saw the tortoise, but she watched it through her spectacles with the fierce stare of a hawk who has just spied a tasty rabbit on the ground below.

Having determined that they could not wait any longer, the priest nodded to the musicians and walked toward the rustic altar followed by Eugene and Mrs. Joyce, who walked arm-in-arm.

"Dearly beloved," said the priest, "we are gathered here today to join Patricia Joyce and Eugene Horace Pook in holy matrimony. We are especially honored to gather here in the very spot on the Matanzas Bay where, more than four hundred years ago, Spanish colonists said the first Catholic Mass on North American soil. Lord, we ask your blessings on this couple and on the children of this new family, who—er—appear to be absent for the moment, but are very much in our hearts and minds."

The gopher tortoise now grazed only a foot away from Mrs. Furbo, completely oblivious to the attack that was about to take place. With a sudden motion, Mrs. Furbo leaned down as if stooping to retrieve a dropped earring and swiftly contained the animal inside her large, cloth handbag—an oversize purse that covered the animal so perfectly that it might have been created explicitly for tortoise catching. Now holding the heavy gopher tortoise in her bag, Mrs. Furbo turned her eyes back to the priest, who was speaking of the shrine of Our Lady of La Leche and the sanctity of marriage.

Captain Jack tapped Mrs. Furbo on the shoulder. "I saw you put that gopher in your bag," he whispered.

"Never you mind," she hissed back.

"That's against the law, ma'am." Captain Jack moved his chair closer, so he was now only a few inches behind Mrs. Furbo.

"Are you a police officer?" Mrs. Furbo kept her eyes on the priest.

"No," said Captain Jack. "I'm a pirate." With a motion every bit as swift and surprising as Mrs. Furbo's attack on the gopher tortoise, Captain Jack seized Mrs. Furbo's handbag. Unfortunately for him, Mrs. Furbo had a surprisingly strong grip on her purse, and the two of them became stuck in an absurd tug-of-war.

Noticing the fight, Evelyn just stared, open-mouthed, and Debbie clapped her hand over her mouth to stifle giggles at the bizarre sight of Captain Jack snatching an elderly woman's purse during a wedding ceremony. Now feeling the priest's eyes on him, Captain Jack gave up and sank back into his seat.

The priest cleared his throat before continuing. "And now," he said, "tradition commands me to raise the question to the friends and relations who have gathered here in support of Eugene and Patty: Is there any one among you who knows *any* reason why these two should not be wed? If so, speak now, or forever hold your peace."

The priest looked out at the faces of the unusually distracted guests: Captain Jack glared at the back of Mrs. Furbo's head; the Furbos both peered down into the handbag; Mary Louise glanced in the direction of Water Street for a sign of her daughter and Gilda, and Evelyn adjusted her parasol-size yellow hat.

Then, across the grass, the priest saw something very strange—a girl wearing an oversize Motor City T-shirt, dirty pajama bottoms, and bare feet ran toward the ceremony as if her very life depended on it. A teenage boy and a younger girl followed her. As Gilda approached, panting, the priest and dumbstruck guests stared at the most inappropriate sight they had ever seen at a St. Augustine wedding.

"Let the record show that the daughter and son of the bride have a very good reason why these two should not be wed," Gilda declared as she made her way toward the altar.

46

The Confession

I had planned a very special reading for this very special day," said Gilda, "an original poem. I had also picked out a far more attractive outfit, including gloves and a hat. However, due to *reasons beyond my control*, I was detained this morning and unable to wear it." Gilda paused to look very directly at Mr. Pook, who appeared to be calculating whether he could run fast enough to get to his car and leave town. Eugene turned to glance behind at the Furbos, who had joined the rest of the guests in glaring at Gilda with as much distaste as they could muster. It was one thing to break up a wedding, but to do so with dirty hair, dusty pajamas, and a Motor City T-shirt was completely unforgivable. "So," Gilda continued, "before I share the reasons that this wedding must not proceed—and they are many—"

"Gilda, what are you doing?!" Mrs. Joyce hissed, having finally found her voice. She stared at her daughter with the horrified relief and boiling anger of a mother whose child has narrowly missed being hit by a car after darting into traffic.

"Believe me, Mom," said Gilda, "you'll want to know what I'm about to tell you."

"Gilda, please get to the point, or *I'm* going to tell them!" said Stephen, who watched from a few feet away.

"Dearly beloved," Gilda began, "the story I am about to tell you would fill many mystery novels—"

"Oh, please, Gilda!" Stephen blurted, "give us the *short* version!"

"I beg your pardon, Stephen, but this is a hard-earned dramatic moment, which you happen to be ruining."

"Fine. *I'll* tell everyone."

Up until now, Mrs. Joyce had watched this exchange between Gilda and Stephen with angry, slack-jawed amazement along with the rest of the wedding guests. Now she suddenly seemed to remember that the two teenagers who were ruining her wedding were actually her own kids.

"Stop it right now!" she shouted, surprising Gilda and Stephen enough that they ceased bickering. "This is unacceptable!" Mrs. Joyce realized that by yelling at her kids in front of everyone, she was only adding further melodrama to a scene that had already spiraled out of control, but she couldn't help it. "First, I can't believe you're late. Second, I can't believe you turned up wearing outfits that I wouldn't even wear to clean the house! Third, you're both grounded for a year!"

"Mom!" Stephen raised his hand in the air. "First, I'll be in college, so I don't think you'll be able to ground me."

"Don't be so sure about that—"

"Mom, I can explain!"

As Gilda, Stephen, and Mrs. Joyce shouted back and forth, Captain Jack seized the opportunity to attempt a tortoise rescue. He gingerly reached under Mrs. Furbo's chair until he grasped her handbag, then slowly pulled the bag toward him. He was just about to free the captive animal when Mrs. Furbo noticed the disappearing bag and jumped up from her seat just in time to grab a handle and pull with all her might.

The tug-of-war between Captain Jack and Mrs. Furbo resumed in full force, this time with such energy that Mrs. Furbo kicked Captain Jack in the shin.

"Ow!" he yelled.

"Please! Everyone be seated!" The priest raised his hands, struggling to capture the attention of the bickering wedding guests. It was a lost cause; by now the entire group was out of control.

Amidst all the chaos, Eugene decided to make a run for it and escape while the getting was good.

But as he tiptoed away from the ridiculous fiasco that had started as his wedding, something very strange happened. Without warning, it began to rain. Next, and just as abruptly, Eugene found himself staring into the dead face of Charlotte, who wore the same wedding dress she had worn on the night of her death.

The guests jumped up to run for cover from the rain. They turned from their seats just in time to see a large man fainting at his own wedding.

"It was me," Eugene muttered as his knees buckled. "I did it. I killed my Charlotte!"

47

Eugene's Story

It rained like a monsoon on the last night I saw Charlotte alive. Come to think of it, the storm was similar to the one we had just this week—tree branches down all over the place. . . . We know how rain comes almost every day and leaves as quickly as it showed up, but this rain was different. I remember how it continued through the whole night.

It was the eve of my wedding, so I wasn't expecting to see Charlotte until the next morning at the ceremony. I thought she was acting a little peculiar at the wedding rehearsal, but I guessed it was just nerves. I was worried, though, because I had heard a few rumors. In those days, people had a way of talking. And Charlotte—well, anything she did seemed to attract people's attention.

I did my best not to think about it. After all, Charlotte's father had just given me the best gift of my life—a beautifully carved antique rifle. I sat up at the dining-room table cleaning that rifle like Mr. Furbo had taught me, and I thought about how he and Mrs. Furbo had welcomed me into the family.

So who suddenly comes into the house looking like something a dog pulled out of a river but Charlotte. Well, I knew something was very wrong if she was barefoot and wearing her mama's silk wedding dress out in the rain on the night before her wedding.

"I have something to tell you, Eugene," she says to me. And then she tells me that she can't marry me—that she loves someone else. She told me she was leaving for good.

Suddenly, it was like I was a little boy again, standing outside in the rain and just looking at them empty train tracks, wondering why my daddy left. *Not this time,* I told myself. This time, I wasn't going to stand for it.

"I'll kill him before I let him take you away," I told Charlotte. "I'll follow him to Europe if I have to."

Well, this upset Charlotte somethin' terrible, and she grabbed the gun by the barrel and tried to take it away from me. It went off, and she fell. I couldn't believe it; she had been shot right in the heart.

I lay next to Charlotte's body for the whole night, just listening to the rain. Well—I suppose I got up just one time, to forge some of her good-bye letters, including a letter to her boyfriend Chance—to tell him that she wanted him to leave without her.

I knew I should call the police, but how could I face Charlotte's parents after what I had done? How could I tell them that I had killed their only daughter, even if it was an accident? Besides, I knew they would make me give Charlotte up; I would have to bury her deep in the ground where I could never be close to her again.

I had decided I would never tell a soul. I would keep Charlotte near me always.

48

Still Single, Still a Doofus

Dressed in jeans, a St. Augustine T-shirt, and a scraggly ponytail, Gilda's mother looked more like her old self than she had since Mr. Pook had started influencing her.

Gilda, on the other hand, was dressed in a lavender vintage dress and a matching hat that she had swiped from one of the closets in Eugene's house. After being locked in a musty old cistern and forced to sit next to a coffin containing a dead body for hours—not to mention several more hours of questioning at the police station after Eugene turned himself in—Gilda felt entitled to take at least one souvenir from the house.

Realizing she hadn't yet updated Wendy on her successful investigation, she took out her notebook and scribbled a letter to be mailed upon landing in Detroit:

Dear Wendy,
    Let's just say that a few teensy things happened since our brief conversation a couple days ago.
    Right now I'm on the plane returning home with Mom and Stephen.

Yes, Stephen is still single, and still a doofus. And no, he didn't kiss that girl I told you about, so you can stop asking. In fact, he literally had one of the worst Halloween nights of his entire life. We both did. To be honest, we're lucky we <u>survived</u> it, so next time you're jealous, just be careful what you wish on people!

I'll fill you in on exactly what happened later, but the result is that Mom did NOT get married. And no, it wasn't because I ruined the wedding either. Okay, technically I <u>did</u> interrupt the actual ceremony, but the reason the wedding got called off was that we all happened to discover something horribly tacky in Mr. Pook's background. (That's how we Southern belles talk about little social faux pas like murders and hidden bodies, by the way.)

After Mr. Pook confessed and turned himself in to the police for questioning, I gave the Furbos the diary I found in Eugene's cistern; it belonged to their daughter (she's the one Eugene killed in case you're not following me here, Wendy). They took the diary and just nodded at me blankly; they seemed to be in shock. It's strange how, even though the Furbos willingly broke off their relationship with Charlotte twenty years ago, now that they know she's actually dead and that she never even got to Europe, you'd think she had just disappeared yesterday. I guess deep down, they must have always assumed that they would see her again someday.

They were completely stunned at this horrible revelation, and just sat there holding the diary and glaring at Eugene. Mrs. Furbo didn't even notice when a gopher tortoise crawled out of her handbag! (Captain Jack told me later that she had tried to kidnap it.)

Speaking of Captain Jack, one benefit of this whole fiasco (and let's face it, as weddings go, it really was one of the biggest disasters in St. Augustine history) is that we now have an invitation to come back and visit him and go on his pirate ship again. He also helped take my mom's mind off the fact that her fiancé had been storing a corpse under his kitchen by taking us out on his boat and singing some of the sea chanteys he knows.

NOTE TO SELF: try to help Mom meet more zoologist-pirates.

Okay, Wendy, get your purple hair dye and lipstick ready, and put away your homework, because I'm coming back to town. And yes—I'm coming back TO STAY!

"I can't believe I didn't make it to the beach even once," Stephen complained.

"Wait a minute." Gilda stopped writing and turned to face Stephen more directly. "Is that all you can say after everything we've been through?"

"I'm just saying; I wish I had gone to the beach."

"Okay, but let me ask you this: Has this experience finally opened your eyes to the reality of ghosts and psychic phenomena?"

"It definitely opened my eyes to the fact that Eugene Pook is one very messed up guy."

Gilda rolled her eyes. "What about you, Mom? Didn't you notice anything strange about Mr. Pook's house?"

"Well, now that you mention it, I did have some odd little spells I couldn't explain."

"What do you mean?" Gilda suddenly remembered how her mother had stood in the middle of the kitchen motionless, as if in a trance. She remembered how her mother's eyes had looked different—as if some other entity was looking through her.

"It was strange. I would walk into a room and immediately forget where I was and what I was doing. And now that I think about it, it often happened in the kitchen—right over that old cistern you and Stephen discovered. . . ." Mrs. Joyce's voice shook at the macabre memory, and she took a deep breath to compose herself. "Anyway, I suppose I did experience some strange events."

"Next time, you should pay more attention to the messages you're getting, Mom," Gilda suggested. "Maybe carry a little notebook in your purse like I do."

"I'm not planning a repeat of this experience, Gilda."

"That's exactly why you need to work on your psychic skills. You'll be able to spot warning signs and trust your intuition better so you don't end up getting engaged to someone who stores his ex-girlfriends under the house again."

"Spotting warning signs would be a good thing," Mrs. Joyce agreed, wryly.

"You're trying to get *Mom* involved in that psychic nonsense now?"

"Stephen, I'm not trying to get Mom involved in anything. I'm guessing Mom has some psychic sensitivity, right, Mom? I'm guessing you probably inherited it from Grandmother McDoogle, just like me."

"I thought Grandmother McDoogle had dementia," Stephen commented.

"Eventually she did," said Mrs. Joyce, "but when she was younger, she had an uncanny knack for predicting all sorts of things that came true. And a lot of her friends believed that she really did speak with ghosts."

"So now you and Gilda are going to sit around the house talking to ghosts?"

"What's wrong with that?" Gilda imagined sitting on the couch with her mother drinking sweet tea, eating chocolate chip cookies, and chatting about local ghost stories like Darla and her mother.

"I just want to find out how crazy things are going to get before I bring any new friends over," Stephen commented.

"Don't worry; I don't have the stomach for this psychic stuff the way your sister does."

"But wouldn't it be fun to learn at least a *little* bit about it, Mom?"

"Well." Mrs. Joyce had always thought of herself as a down-to-earth person—someone who didn't have time for impractical pursuits. She had certainly never considered herself a particularly intuitive, creative, or psychic person. *But what if these things really do run in families?* she thought. *And what if I showed a little interest? Maybe Gilda and I might feel like we have something in common for a change.* "Okay, why not?" she said. "Maybe you can invite Wendy over and we'll have a little psychic party, since the two of you didn't get to go trick-or-treating this year."

"Oh, great! I'll tell Wendy; she'll be so excited."

Is it possible that I'm actually excited about doing something with my mother? Gilda wondered as she added a note about the psychic party to her letter. *I guess the embarrassing answer is yes.*

Gilda sat happily between her mother and brother for the rest of the flight and didn't even mind when Stephen bumped her elbow off the armrest for the fifth time in a row. If there was one thing she had come to realize during the past few days, it was that she was grateful for the family she had, despite the many flaws, quirks, and embarrassing scenes that came with it.

49

Psychic Sisters

Dear Gilda:

I hope you're doing well up in Michigan.

I just wanted to thank you again for letting me borrow your <u>Master Psychic's Handbook</u>; I read the whole thing and even took down notes, so I'm sending it back to you now. I think meeting you and reading this book really helped me feel less scared of the things I see. Now I create a "boundary" to protect myself, and also try to analyze the situation more so I can learn something from everything that happens to me. I also light my guardian angel candle every night and say a prayer for everyone I care about, and I haven't had as many nightmares since.

I thought you would be interested to know that I saw a light on inside Mr. Pook's house the other night, so of course I thought of Charlotte's ghost. I looked over the fence, and I realized it was Mr. Furbo sitting there all by himself. He looked really sad, so I went over to talk to him. He was sitting there reading that diary you found—the one Charlotte kept. And it kind of looked like he had been crying, but I wasn't sure.

Well, I ended up telling him that I live next door and that I used to see the ghost of his daughter around—and that I hadn't seen her ever since her body was found. He was really interested. He told me that he thought it was all his fault she died because if he hadn't told her to go away just because he didn't like her new boyfriend, she might still be alive.

I kind of had a feeling that there was a message Charlotte wanted to tell him—so I tried to tune into it the way the Psychic's Handbook instructs you to do.

"I think Charlotte wants to tell you something, Mr. Furbo," I said. "I feel like she's at peace now," I told him. "I really do. And she isn't even mad at you—or at anyone—anymore. But she says you're supposed to do something in her memory."

"What kind of thing?" he asked me. He was really listening to me, as if I had all the answers in the world! And then I got this picture in my mind of Mr. Furbo and a family named Owens sharing their datil-pepper recipes at the next barbecue festival. "Mr. Furbo," I said, "Charlotte thinks you might feel better if you went and got to know the family of that boyfriend she had so many years ago."

So Mr. Furbo, he just stared at me, and then he nodded as if he was thinking about that idea really seriously. "Maybe so," he said. "Maybe I'll just do that."

Anyways, Gilda, I hope you'll come visit us here in St. Augustine again. Mama says I can maybe come up to see you in Michigan sometime, too, although not in winter because I wouldn't have a warm enough coat for this time of year.

Your friend and fellow "psychic sister"! ☺
Darla

50

The Eyes of the Dead

Looking like a character out of a vampire movie with her Goth-inspired black lipstick, heavy eyeliner, and traditional colonial costume, Tina led her tour group of rowdy kids down Water Street in the moonlight. The kids had just visited the Old Fort and heard the story of the headless ghost of the famous Seminole Indian leader Osceola; they were now prone to fits of giggling and screaming as they made their way through the dark city neighborhoods of St. Augustine.

Following Tina's swinging lantern, they walked toward the house that had given birth to the latest ghost tale—the tragic, macabre love story that had the whole city talking, gossiping, and embellishing.

"You may have heard the news stories of an alleged murder that took place at this house," said Tina, facing her charges in front of the haunted property. "You should know that it's also a ghost story." She turned to look at the crime-scene tape draping the front porch and the blocked-off section of the lawn where archaeologists had begun excavating the property. "This story is one of my favorites because I actually met some of the people who were involved.

"Once upon a time," Tina began, "a man named Eugene Pook fell in love with a local woman named Charlotte Furbo. They shared a love for antiques, and Eugene particularly loved the antiques that Charlotte had inherited from her family—a family with deep Minorcan roots in St. Augustine. The two of them started an antiques business called Charlotte's Attic, and everything was great at first.

"But pretty soon, it became clear that Eugene and Charlotte were very different. Eugene loved traditional things; Charlotte wanted to experiment. They argued about how to run the business. Gradually, they drifted apart and Charlotte had an affair with an African-American serviceman who was about to be stationed overseas. Well, when Eugene heard about Charlotte's plan to leave him, he basically went crazy. Some say he shot her on purpose; some believe his story that it was an accident. Anyway, he killed his fiancée, and then he hid her body in an old cistern beneath the house.

"Well, it was Charlotte's murder that seemed to awaken some kind of dark magic in the house. The neighbors began to see spirits walking around the property—especially the apparition of a woman wearing a white bridal gown.

"After many years, Eugene decided to get married, and who did he pick? A woman who looked very much like Charlotte—the woman he had murdered long ago. He even dressed his new fiancée in his dead fiancée's vintage clothes.

"But pretty soon, his fiancée became suspicious of some of the strange things going on in Mr. Pook's old house. She often heard mysterious calls for help that seemed to come from beneath the floor of the kitchen.

"It was on Halloween night—the night before Mr. Pook was to be married to his new bride—that his new fiancée's children made a chilling discovery: the body of Charlotte Furbo was lying in an old casket beneath Mr. Pook's house. Not surprisingly, the wedding that was supposed to take place the next morning was called off at the last minute.

"As for Eugene—well, you can read about his court trial in the papers.

"For now, this old house stands empty. The only people who come here are the archaeologists who are in the process of conducting an excavation. You see, they've discovered that there's an ancient Timucua Indian burial ground here.

"But every now and then, neighbors say they see a light go on inside this house in the middle of the night even though nobody lives here now. And every Halloween night—especially on ones when there's a big fall rainstorm—you might spot a woman dressed in white opening the front door of the house. Sometimes she carries an old suitcase, as if she's ready to flee somewhere. But the moment she steps out of the house to find her freedom, she always disappears."

Swinging her lantern, Tina walked down the sidewalk, heading back in the direction of the waterfront and the Castillo. She looked forward to the end of the tour when she could head out to Scarlett O'Hara's pub to meet her friends.

Nobody in the group glanced behind. Nobody saw the eyes of the dead watching them from the darkened house on Water

Street—the Civil War soldiers with their eternally bleeding wounds and the dark, watching faces of the Timucuan ghost families. The ghosts knew that tour guides would get their stories all wrong as time passed until the stories themselves would become ghosts. Only their bones would tell the truth—the bones of the old and young who rest together on their sacred ground.

Acknowledgments

Gilda's curiosity and openness to new experiences always leads her to investigate fascinating places, and this fifth book in the series is no exception. *In The Bones of the Holy*, Gilda explores "the nation's oldest city"—St. Augustine, Florida. During the writing process, I was inspired by my interviews with people of all walks of life in St. Augustine: Through our conversations, many local ghost stories and tall tales emerged along with detailed oral histories about the region. A common thread was the genuine passion these individuals feel for their very special city and its diverse cultural influences. I am grateful to every individual who took the time to share his or her memories and perspectives: In particular, Mary Ballinger, teacher extraordinaire at Ketterlinus Elementary School, deserves special recognition for introducing me to a long list of extremely interesting and helpful individuals, including her colleagues Linda Barnes, Michael Sharman, Elizabeth Marsh, Suzanne

Fraser, and Denise Droege. Special thanks are also due to Linda Barnes, an outstanding educator who generously shared the fruits of her own extensive research into local oral histories and her knowledge of Minorcan history in St. Augustine. Several "genuine Minorcans," including Larry and MaryEllen Masters and Sandy Craig, founder of Ghost Tours of St. Augustine, generously took the time to illuminate many historical details and share personal anecdotes. Thanks are also due to several professional ghost tour guides, including the very spooky and also hilarious Andrew Nance, who scared the daylights out of me with his great stories on the Schooner Freedom.

One thing became clear in St. Augustine: Almost everyone has a ghost story or two to tell. I would like to thank several delightful ladies for their hospitality and also for sharing their own fascinating stories: Dr. Margaret Finnegan, owner of the historic St. Francis Inn; Laura Puckett and her daughter Blake; Laura McCracken and her daughters; and Mary Alice Hayes and her family.

Thank you to St. Johns County Archaeologist Robin Moore, who shared his expertise and explained numerous details about his intriguing field of study in St. Augustine.

Finally, in an era when we often hear that editing is a "dying art," I have been fortunate to work with some genuinely outstanding and insightful editors. I am extremely grateful to Andrew Harwell, Maureen Sullivan, Lauri Hornik, and Rosanne Lauer at Penguin who helped make this book possible with their hard work and support. Thanks also to all the friends and family members who helped with aspects of research or the manuscript along the way, especially my aunt Nancy Pegg; my father, Professor Kenneth Brostrom; fellow writers Carolyn Parkhurst and Anne McCallum; and my agent, Doug Stewart.

Turn the page for a chapter
of the first book in the series…

GILDA JOYCE
Psychic Investigator

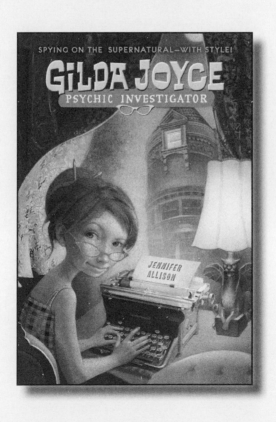

1

It's Not a Lie If It Comes True

In the back row of Mrs. Weinstock's eighth-grade English classroom, Gilda Joyce chewed on a lock of her dark hair and pretended to listen as her classmates described their plans for the summer on the last day of the school year. Gilda paid little attention to the discussion, because she was secretly absorbed in reading a small, dog-eared book called *The Master Psychic's Handbook: A Guide to Psychic Principles and Methods*. Ever since she'd found the book at a garage sale, Gilda had been a big fan of the author, Master Psychic Balthazar Frobenius, who had grown up in one of the most dangerous neighborhoods in Detroit and who claimed to have used his psychic gifts to help detectives solve numerous crimes.

As the other students chattered about visiting places like Lake Michigan or Florida or the caves of Kentucky, Gilda perused a chapter entitled "Following Impulses, No Matter How Illogical," in which Dalthazar Frobenius explained how psychics sometimes get distinct physical sensations:

> . . . impulses that seem arbitrary at the time, but which actually lead to some fortuitous event or crucial piece of information. For example, a psychic might suddenly experience a craving for an unusual food that leads her to a neighborhood that she would never visit under normal circumstances. What does she discover in this neighborhood besides food? *Most likely a person seeking the help of her psychic abilities or a clue leading to the resolution of an unsolved crime.*
>
> For the psychic, it is often the *unexpected impulse* that leads her to - people in need of help, clues that solve crimes, and even spirits seeking her attention.
>
> Over time, you will recognize your own physical cues: you may have headaches, itches, aches, twitches, or other physical sensations that become your own personal signals—a kind of *psychic radar* that helps you perceive important information.

As she read the passage, Gilda felt an unusual itch in her left ear. She wondered whether this might be one of her own physical signals that she was about to have a paranormal experience.

Gilda glanced up from her book and realized that Mrs. Weinstock was looking at her.

"Gilda, how about you? What are *your* plans for the summer?"

At the moment, her only specific plan was to spend much of the summer spying on a strikingly unattractive young man she had nicknamed "Plaid Pants" who worked at a nearby convenience store, but she didn't want to admit this to Mrs. Weinstock. Remembering that her mother had recently spoken of her eccentric cousin who lived in California, Gilda blurted the first idea that came to mind. "I'm going to San Francisco," she said.

Everyone in the room turned to gaze at her with a combination of surprise and curiosity, causing Gilda to immediately regret the impulsive lie.

"And what will you be doing there? A vacation with your family?"

"I'll be writing a novel." Why did she tell Mrs. Weinstock that?

Gilda's pale, freckled complexion turned pink with embarrassment, and Mrs. Weinstock peered at her suspiciously. Gilda had been known to make up stories in the past, and she knew Mrs. Weinstock regarded most of her comments with a degree of skepticism. "Writing a novel is a pretty ambitious plan for a girl your age."

Mrs. Weinstock obviously didn't want to believe that an eighth grader could write a novel, even if it was Gilda, who had a unique talent for writing in a voice well beyond her years. In fact, because Gilda had used vocabulary words like *specious* and *trenchant* in some of her assignments, Mrs.

1

Weinstock had unfairly hinted that she thought Gilda had plagiarized on several occasions.

"I've already written a few novels," Gilda replied, "so it's no big deal." This statement was partly true; her bedroom closet was stuffed with bizarre stories that she hoped would someday make her famous.

"How interesting," said Mrs. Weinstock, crossing her arms over her chest. "Do tell us more."

Gilda chewed on her pencil, trying to think of something to say that would make Mrs. Weinstock and the entire class stop looking at her as if she were a toad that had suddenly explained it enjoyed singing opera.

After a few agonizing seconds, Gilda was saved by the last school bell of the year, immediately followed by the clatter of students rushing toward the door and fleeing the building.

As Gilda trudged down the hallway, she felt irritated with herself. Was her impulsive idea of traveling to San Francisco the product of a genuine psychic impulse, or was it merely a compulsive lie? Lately, Gilda had been making a genuine effort to tell the truth. At least, she had promised herself that if she *did* tell a spontaneous lie, she would do everything possible to make the lie actually come true. In order to maintain this resolution, she would now have to find a way to get herself from Michigan to San Francisco for the summer—a plan that suddenly seemed entirely impossible, given the fact that she had no money and that her mother would almost certainly veto the idea.

"Hey, *since when* are you going to San Francisco?!" Gilda turned to face her best friend, Wendy Choy, who was struggling under the weight of an enormous blue backpack.

"Look, Wendy, you're going to music camp, right? Do I ask you a million questions about that?"

"Yes, you do. And I'm only asking because—well, you know how you *are.*"

"If you don't believe I'm going to San Francisco," said Gilda, "just call my mom and ask." Gilda knew that Wendy would never call her mother. Wendy hated getting stuck in conversations with Mrs. Joyce.

"But just *yesterday* you told me that you were planning to spend a few months spying on Plaid Pants at the convenience store," Wendy persisted. "You said you thought he might be a serial killer."

"I wouldn't waste my time doing something that dumb," Gilda lied. In truth, Gilda had been looking forward to spying on Plaid Pants, particularly since she had just made two interesting discoveries: (1) Plaid Pants had a real name—Hector Flack (a name Gilda found far more scandalous than the nickname she had given him), and (2) Hector/Plaid Pants had recently gotten in trouble for eating candy on the job. Gilda thought he might be in danger of getting fired.

Lately, however, Gilda sensed that Wendy had lost interest in the "neighborhood surveillance" project they had started after reading *Harriet the Spy* back in elementary school. Wendy also seemed uninterested in the business she and Gilda had been planning to start—Psychic Investigations Inc. While Gilda had been diligently working to develop her psychic abilities, Wendy seemed increasingly skeptical about the whole enterprise. Besides, Wendy would be spending three months at a music camp in northern Michigan, leaving Gilda on her own all summer for the first time.

"Do you want to come over and spy on Plaid Pants just one *last* time before the summer?" Gilda ventured. "Or how about conducting a séance? We haven't done any psychic investigations for ages—"

"I can't. I've got to start packing for camp, and I haven't practiced piano nearly enough this week. We can't play these games forever, you know. We're almost in ninth grade!"

"Wendy, they aren't games; they're *careers.*"

"Maybe for *you,* but some of us have to live in the real world."

Gilda felt deflated. Wendy was abandoning her, and the real world was such a bore.

As Gilda exited the front doors of the school, she vowed that she would find a way to get herself to San Francisco. *Maybe there was a* reason *I blurted out that idea of going to San Francisco,* Gilda thought. *Maybe it really was a psychic impulse.*